Past and Present

Past and Present

Rosemary Johnson

Bridge House

British Library Cataloguing in Publication Data
A Record of this Publication is available from the British
Library

ISBN 978-1-914199-94-3

This edition published 2025 by Bridge House Publishing
Manchester, England

Contents

Introduction

When I first read about the opportunity to put together a single author collection, I supposed I would have to pass because, surely, I hadn't written 30,000 plus words in short fiction. Then I browsed the files on my computer and got a surprise.

I tend to take my fiction ideas from the world around us. You know the old adage: write about what you know. I enjoy comedy, in written and televised form, so this collection starts with humorous stories and then moves on to stories set in the past. For me, historical fiction is not about young women in long frocks seeking husbands or acts of derring-do. Some authorities say that the action in a story must have taken place at least fifty years ago for it to be classed as 'historical', whereas my view is that, if the piece has obvious links to a particular period, it qualifies. Settings for my 'historicals' range from Biblical times through to the fall of Communism in Eastern Europe and Brexit. Some of the historical stories are also comedic – we shouldn't always take ourselves too seriously. The collection then moves on to the present day.

Enjoy the read.

Rosemary Johnson
2025

An Important Call

'Your call is important to us. It has been placed in a queue.' The voice at the end of the phone sounds like a machine and probably is one.

I say nothing.

I'm just settling into listening to *Greensleeves* when it cuts in again. 'Calls may be recorded for training and quality purposes.'

More *Greensleeves* then Handel's *Water Music*, played on something weird, panpipes possibly. I tap out the rhythm on my desk.

'All our call-centre operatives are busy at the moment.'

I reach for my mug, only to remember that I finished my coffee some time ago. *Do machines take tea breaks?*

'We are experiencing an exceptionally high volume of calls at this time.'

You don't say? Now I'm getting a signature-tune to some television programme from the 1980s. *What was it now?*

'Customers are respectfully requested to check that appliances are connected to the power supply.'

Yes, yes, yes. I know that story about the bloke (or woman) who swore his (or her) printer didn't work and found he (or she) hadn't switched it on. But I'm not an idiot. My issue is real. I click my mouse several times. Still nothing's happening on my screen. I need to speak to someone, a proper human being.

Still that awful theme tune. *What was that programme?* All I can recall is that I didn't like it. And I don't want to hear it now. *Come on. Speak to me.*

'Answers to many frequently asked questions are available on our website.'

Yes, yes, you stupid machine, but what good is that to

me? Come on. Where are you, you terribly busy call-centre operatives? I don't believe you're there at all. Or that you even exist.

Not *Greensleeves* again. I'm going to complain. On Facebook, on X and all the other social media. I'll write to the local paper. I'll contact my MP, the Prime Minister even. He needs to know that people in this country have stopped talking to each other.

'Good afternoon, caller. How can I help you today?'

'Right. At last. I've got no internet.'

'No internet, madam?'

'Yes. I mean, no. No internet. I need you to send someone round—'

'We don't deal with internet queries here, madam. You'll need to log your service request through our website.'

How?

Bachelor Boy

'I'm not sleeping well. In fact, I don't think anybody in Little Wobblemarsh has had a decent night's sleep since he arrived,' said Sylvia.

Her custom was to take herself up to bed at ten thirty prompt with a hot water bottle and a good book. Born Miss Sylvia Singleton sixty years ago, she had come to accept that she would never be Mrs Anything Else.

'The sounds of the countryside, we're used to,' she went on. 'Cockerels, sheep, cows, even combine harvesters driving up and down all night with their headlights on, but not a peacock screeching at four o'clock in the morning.'

'Peacocks are not native to East Anglia,' said Dorothy, who considered herself an expert on feathered friends since she'd joined the *Essex Wildlife Trust*.

Village residents agreed that somebody ought to say something, but nobody liked to, bearing in mind to whom the big bird belonged. In spite of everything, he was a decent old stick, their MP.

'The postman says it's blue all over and absolutely huge.' Dorothy held out her hands. 'As wide as this.'

'Size and colour are not the issues,' said Sylvia. 'This is a noise nuisance and a matter for the Parish Council.'

'Er... well.'

'The Parish Council, dear. You're the Chair and you should have a word with him.'

Nothing happened.

'I will speak it to him,' said Sylvia a few weeks later, when she and Dorothy were enjoying a glass of sherry in Sylvia's house one evening. 'Seems nobody else is going to.'

'You, dear?'

'Yes. Me. Sylvia. The unfortunate person who lives

next door to our dear Right Hon and hears that terrible screeching the loudest.'

'Yes, but you can't just knock on our MP's door and tell him to get rid of his peacock,' said Dorothy.

'I have an idea.'

When Sylvia explained what she had in mind, her friend frowned. 'It wouldn't work. We've never done fortune-telling at the village fete before.' The Parish Council Chair, whose role included organising this glorious annual event, stood up and reached for her handbag. 'I think it's time I went, dear.'

'You're forgetting the church garden party last summer.' Sylvia did not move from her chair. 'He had his tea leaves read by Mina the Mystic three times. You and I were on refreshments and we had to keep brewing up for him.'

'Huh. Mina's dress left nothing to the imagination. Men, they're all the same.'

As usual the fete took place in the grounds of the MP's house. The stallholders were still setting up when Sylvia arrived wearing a purple and yellow tie-and-dye skirt, looped earrings and lots of scarves. 'From the charity shop,' she said to Dorothy in a confidential whisper.

'I can see that,' her friend said aloud.

'Now, where's my tent? Already the fortune-teller outfit was making her feel hot.

'Over there. Next to bric-a-brac.'

Sylvia cast her eye around. Ancient trestle tables from the village hall, pressed into service just once a year for probably fifty years, were being erected around the Right Hon's garden, their rickety legs squeaking in protest, as if they knew the damage they were about to do his immaculate lawn. She noted the bric-a-brac stall, already loaded with its usual stock of crockery and ornaments dating from the 1970s, many of which reappeared year after year. Then she saw what was next to it. 'No, Dorothy, no. Surely not that thing?'

Dorothy harumphed. 'I think it's very kind of the Hendersons to lend it to us. Especially as they're going camping in Norfolk with their grandchildren tomorrow.'

'How am I going to be a mysterious clairvoyant from inside that... that... candy bar?

However, soon there was a long queue of people waiting outside the custard yellow and baby pink stripy canvas, eager with their one pound pieces. All to a good cause, of course: the upkeep of Little Wobblemarsh Village Hall. 'I can see your daughter in a gown and hood,' the clairvoyant with a familiar local accent told several punters. 'You're standing on the deck of a big ship. Could it be a cruise liner?' Sylvia, who devoured romantic novels every evening, had no trouble making up the sorts of fortunes people would like to hear.

She'd been sitting there for two hours when she saw what she wanted to see: two manicured fingers and a distinctive signet ring around the entry flap. 'Just going to have my fortune told, darling,' he said to his wife, in that booming voice, capable of filling the chamber of the House of Commons.

Sylvia sat bolt upright in her garden chair. This was her moment.

But Mrs Right Hon was tut-tutting. 'Load of nonsense. I want to look at produce. I hear they have some of that nice quince jam again.'

'Very well, darling.'

Sylvia groaned into her 'crystal' ball. 'You've got to get him in here,' she said when Dorothy brought in the free cup of tea and cake to which all stall-holders were entitled.

The Parish Council Chair arched her brow. 'Sylvia, this was never going to work.'

'At least I'm trying.'

Minutes later, the signet ring reappeared. The Right Hon strutted in, lifting his feet in slow deliberate steps, like a peacock himself, and placing two digits to his mouth. He stared at her as he sat down in the sagging canvas-bottomed chair opposite Sylvia. 'You're not Mina the Mystic?'

'No.'

He leant forward to peer at the small portion of her face not submerged in scarves. 'Mrs Singleton, isn't it?'

'Miss.'

'Oh.'

'If you'd like me to tell your fortune, it's one pound.'

'Of course.' His money clinked on the saucer.

Sylvia had everything prepared. She told him he was going on a long journey to a faraway place, taking with him something blue.

He frowned, ridges forming on his forehead like the speed bumps on the road outside, something for which the Parish Council had campaigned for over ten years. 'You mean I should leave the Conservative Party? He shook his head. 'Couldn't do that, dear lady. The Leader wouldn't like it.'

Sylvia, who'd anticipated this, pointed again to her 'crystal' ball, which she had purchased last weekend, 'reduced for quick sale' from B&Q. 'This is in your domestic hemisphere. Something blue at home.'

'Nope. Can't think of anything. My wife likes everything pink.'

'Or even in the garden?'

He was silent for a moment. 'Aha.' He bounded up, knocking his legs against Sylvia's table and nearly knocking her ball on to the grass. 'Hydrangeas. Never liked them. I'm going to pull them up and throw them on the compost heap... at the bottom of the garden. Faraway place. Ha ha.'

Sylvia's shoulders sagged as she watched him disappear through the tent flap. Over the next hour interest in the fortune-teller dwindled to nothing so, while the Right Hon was calling the raffle, she browsed the book stall, even though she herself had donated much of its stock. Chancing upon a battered copy of a paperback entitled *Keeping Peacocks*, she bought it for thirty pence. She was flicking through its brittle brown pages when she became aware of a shadow across the entrance to her stripy tent.

'Oh,' gasped Sylvia.

He halted, one scaled leg raised and claws flexed, as if he were doing yoga. Then he strutted inside, his blue tail feathers trailing behind him like a ball gown with a lace train.

'Oh. You are beautiful.' She had never seen a peacock close-to before.

He clucked, a throaty, resonant cluck which seemed to say that there could be more, that he was turning the volume down for now, but not forever. With his golden plume at a rakish angle, he fixed his eyes upon her.

Lowering her gaze, Sylvia closed her *Keeping Peacocks*. It would be rude to read it in front of him.

Yet the sound of the book closing seemed to unsettle him. All of a sudden, he drew himself to his full height and, with a sound like rustling silk, unfurled his full glory, orange jewels with black centres on a blue mantilla.

She drew in her breath to speak, but anything she might've said would've been drowned by his ear-splitting scream, not once, not twice, but over and over again. 'No,' she cried, slapping her palms over her ears. 'No. Please don't.'

He quietened. Eventually.

'I think I know what your trouble is,' she said holding up the book. 'Believe me, there are times when I've wanted to screech too. But not at four in the morning.' She fixed her gaze upon him. 'That. Must. Stop.'

He tilted his head to one side.

'I'll do what I can. Your problem may be easier to resolve than mine, my beautiful bachelor boy. They say you can find anything on the internet.'

Several days later a small van, with 'Peabody & Son' stencilled on the side, drew up in front of the Right Hon's house. Sylvia watched from her landing window, her fingers very much crossed.

The man himself answered the door. He bent down to look at the big wooden crate which had been deposited on his step and peered through the grille. Sylvia was too far away to see anything properly, but she might have caught a glimpse of brown. The Right Hon studied the delivery note, jabbing it with his finger and shaking his head at the van driver, but MPs can never resist gifts, especially those they wouldn't have to record on the Register of Interests. Then he picked up the crate and carried it around the side of his house and out of sight.

All Sylvia could do now was to wait. She put away the laundry, dusted everywhere upstairs, and she was cleaning the back bedroom window when she saw it at last. Pottering around the Right Hon's garden, reaching down her elegant neck to peck at the ground, was the brown peahen.

'Love at last, my bachelor boy,' whispered Sylvia. 'I said I'd do what I could, didn't I?'

The boy, standing upon a freshly-dug patch of earth where a blue hydrangea used to grow, watched her in silence. The perfect gentleman.

That night Little Wobblemarsh slept.

Unaccustomed as I Am

'Ladies and gentlemen, Laura and Barry, it is usual for the best man's speech to be... er... slightly risqué. I believe that at some weddings older guests leave beforehand, so as to give the best man a free rein, as it were. However, maiden aunts and old friends of the family need have no worries on this occasion. This is Barry we are talking about.

'I've known our bridegroom, Barry, since we started primary school together just after the war. He won the Good Conduct Prize in the reception class and there were many other awards to follow. We were together at secondary school and later at Cambridge, where he achieved a first in computer science and I... er... didn't do so well, in natural sciences. If you are hoping to hear about racy stories of student life, getting drunk and climbing over college walls at night, I did all that, but without Barry. Barry was the perfect undergraduate, spending most of his time in the computer lab, or making music with the Stradivarius String Quartet, who played for us so delightfully in church this afternoon.

'If you must know, I have searched high and low for some embarrassing stories about Barry, but I have failed. Completely. I even asked Laura and she couldn't think of anything except that he practises his viola too much, especially when she wanted him to do things for the wedding. Surely, even string quartets are naughty? Occasionally. I mean, it's nineteen seventy. We've got mini-skirts, transistor radios, sexual liberation and a few years ago we had the Summer of Love. Being a best man these days is very hard.

'Barry and Laura have bought a house in California and he will continue working over there. To be absolutely frank and honest with you, ladies and gentlemen, I don't understand what Barry does in his job. I know he does something with computers. Computers were always his thing. Programming?... Yes, he's nodding... He told me last night that he and some other... boffins... are working on some... code... and the idea is that they will be able to see on their computer stuff that's on other computers. What do you call it, Barry? The inter thingummy... inter... inter... net?

'Seriously, though, Barry is my best friend and the nicest bloke you could ever hope to meet. Pray be upstanding and drink to the bride and groom.'

Eight O'Clock

All I can hear is the dull thudding of my heart. Already beads of sweat have formed on my forehead. My shoulders are hunched forward, every muscle in my body tight and ready.

I fix my eyes on the clock, watching the minute hand edge, in sharp jolts, towards the twelve at the top.

'Go. Now.'

Susan's words jolt through me like an electric shock, almost making me drop the device in my hands. Not quite, though. I'm jabbing at its buttons. They squeak in protest. The race is on.

Then... nothing. *Please, please, get on with it.*

Burr burr, burr burr. This is promising. This is good.

Burr burr, burr burr. *Answer, answer. I know you're there.*

I clasp the receiver more tightly, as if it might leap from my hand. *Come on, come on. Me, me.* Someone else'll get in front of me – again. I've been waiting for two whole days. Don't they realise I'm sick and in bed?

I hear a click. I draw in my breath. They're picking up. It's happening. I'm getting in there. I exhale like a March wind. Before they can say anything, I start to talk. Everything I've wanted to say over three days pours out of me in a torrent.

Silence.

I cough, to remind them I'm here.

Another click. 'All our appointments for today are booked,' says the voice – or is it a machine? 'Please call back at eight o'clock tomorrow.'

I would've thrown the receiver against the wall, watched its plastic components wrench open and smash, but at that moment Susan pokes her head around the bedroom door. 'Did you get through to the doctor, dear?'

17

Penny Carter is Unwell

Penny awoke early. With the morning sun streaming through the office windows, she hummed to herself as she tidied her desktop and put her files into folders. But today it was a real effort to get started, and she didn't feel her usual energy, even at the touch of Greg's silken fingers.

'Maybe I have a virus,' she thought.

That evening she visited Dr Norton. In his turquoise bow-tie and flapping white coat, she thought he was quite the genuine article, until he said, 'We'll have to take your top off.'

She didn't like this one bit. As he groped around looking for leads, she asked, 'Is it my memory, Doctor?'

'Unlikely.' He peered over his half-moon glasses. 'I hope you're not using that stuff off the internet.'

'But it's free, Doctor.'

'You're just run down. What you need is lots of fresh air and plenty of exercise.'

But next day Greg told her that she was slow. The shame of it. Then he shoved his memory stick into one of the new laptops and printed his sales brochure on her colour printer, the one she was quite attached to. She needed to see another doctor. She contacted Dr McAfee this time.

'Doctor, I'm so worried.'

Dr McAfee's red beard clashed with his pink shirt. 'Aye.'

'Is it my age, Doctor?'

He shook his head as he looked through her history. 'None of us are getting any younger, dear.'

'I've heard some terrible things.' Penny went black, then white, then black again. 'In some offices they replace all hardware on a three-year rolling programme. I can still see the look on that inkjet printer when they carried him away. He was only two and a half.'

'Wouldn't happen now. Budgets are tighter these days.'

Penny's fan whirred in relief.

'What you need is a good clear out.'

'Oh. The little orange sachets? I order them for Greg online.' She adjusts her volume to a whisper. 'Quite embarrassing.'

'Same sort of thing. We call it a defrag.'

'Will it hurt?'

'No, no. I'm just going to rearrange your files and folders—'

'I do that myself, every morning.'

'Let me explain. I'm going to push them closer together to make more space.' He arched his eyebrows. 'Your Greg should do this for you every six months.'

'Greg's forgetful, Doctor.'

'You'll feel like a new woman afterwards.'

The following morning Greg rushed into the office, crying, 'Penny. Quick. Mr Large wants to see the sales presentation. He's coming now.'

'Okay, okay.' She rushed to open PowerPoint.

'As fast as you can. Please, Penny. I know you haven't been yourself but…'

'I'm fine, thank you, Greg. There you are.'

'Oh, well done, Penny.'

'The New York office must see this,' said Mr Large, after she had whizzed through slides, animations and videos.

She booked Greg's business class flight and luxury Manhattan hotel. If only she were a notebook, she could go with him.

Daniel and the Pussycats

She expected him to be more discreet. In the circumstances. Yet there he was as usual, stretched across the floor, backside in the air, nose to the carpet and facing Jerusalem. With the window open. 'God of our fathers, God of Abraham, God of Isaac, hear your servant, Daniel.'

She sneaked a glance at the street below. 'Dad. Don't. Please.'

His gold and silver jewellery jangled around his wrists as he drew himself into a sitting position. 'Judith.' He was speaking in his dead serious voice, the one he used when telling her not to speak to strangers. 'I'm praying for the freedom of the Children of Israel.'

'Dad, puh-leese... Not now. Not after King Darius's decree.'

He raised one eyebrow. 'What decree?'

'About not praying to any other gods except him.'

'Now my little Judy doesn't need to worry her pretty little head about Darius and his decrees.' He pulled himself to his feet.

'But he's put it in writing, in accordance with the law of the Medes and Persians, which...'

'...Cannot be changed. Yeah, yeah, yeah.'

'Dad, you'll get thrown to the lions.'

He laughed as he slipped his feet into his leather sandals. 'Will I heck?'

'It's only for thirty days, Dad. Can't you not pray for thirty days?'

'Office politics, Pet. I work for His Majesty. I know how these things work. It's all done to impress the satraps and the other administrators. And they, my little flower, report to me.' He leaned over to kiss her cheek. 'Off to work I go.'

'Mum would've told you not to. Dad, this praying, it's dangerous.'

'I am not putting myself in any danger, my little flower. And your mother, bless her, was of the tribe of Benjamin. She feared the Lord.' He wagged his finger at their daughter. 'She would've done the same.'

'No, she would not.' *If my mum had been alive,* thought Judith as he left, *he would've listened to her.*

He was doing it again at midday, farting as he prostrated himself. He'd had a good lunch.

That afternoon Judith hung out with the other girls as usual, but set off for home a bit later than normal, meaning to avoid her dad's next embarrassing pray-in. When she turned the corner into their street, she became aware of a crowd milling around outside their house, but there was always somebody waiting about for Daniel, Darius's right-hand man, wanting him to petition the king about something or other. Two soldiers were leading a man through our gate, his legs in irons and his torso trussed up with rope. *Burglars,* Judith thought. *Not again.*

'Excuse me. Let me through.' But they were making too much noise to hear the calls of a mere girl. 'Please. I live here.' Nobody even turned around. She managed to shove her way into a place where she could see over people's shoulders. She wasn't in the least bothered that she'd lost one of her sandals in the hurly burly. She had plenty of others at home.

The soldiers were nudging the burglar forward with their spears but he wasn't looking in the least ashamed or frightened, as burglars might be expected to. He was actually nodding at the crowd and thanking them for coming, as Judith's dad might've done. 'All a big mistake. See you all later.' He even spoke in Daniel's voice. The

21

evening sun caught his heavy black hair, highlighting every fleck of flint grey and the shiny bald patch on top. *No, no, this couldn't be.*

She attempted to run towards him, throwing out her arms, but the sharp points of the soldiers' spears crashed and clattered, iron upon iron, in front of her. *No, no, this was not really happening.* More words welled up in her throat, tumbling over each other, jamming at the base of her tongue and striking her speechless. Yet, inside her head, 'I told you so, Dad,' rang out loud and clear.

She stood on one leg then the other, the dust and rubble of the street pressing in between her bare toes. *It would be all right, wouldn't it? Daniel, her dad, was important, really important, wasn't he? He'd just call on Darius and explain.* All a big mistake.

'Judith,' he called suddenly across the baying crowd. 'Judith. Go to the palace. Now.'

She stared ahead, her eyes unable to fix on anything, his words jangling in her head without meaning.

'Listen to me, Judith. Go to Darius.'

Behind her the rabble were clapping and chanting in a slow rhythm. 'Lions.' Clap. 'Lions.' Clap. 'Lions.' Clap. 'Ha-ha-ha. Lions.' Clap. 'Lions.' As the soldiers led him away, their cry changed. 'Hebrew.' Clap. 'Jew.' Clap. 'Yid.'

The servants, watching and listening in the courtyard, fell away as she rushed inside. Her father's cloak lay over a chair and his wine cup sat on the table, half-full, as if he were about to come back to drink it. She studied the marble pillars in the hallway, counting them, five on the left and four on the right, then the carpet, following its whirly pattern with her eye. In this city of Babylon where she had lived all her life, she was quite alone.

Someone cleared his throat.

She started, her heart juddering inside her body.

'You'd better get yourself off to the palace, Miss.' It was Hassan, her father's manservant, squatting in the corner.

'Me?'

He said nothing, just sat there.

'I can't.'

'If you don't, I will. Though Darius'll more likely listen to Daniel's daughter than to me, a servant.'

An unnatural stillness hung about the house. Silence has its own sound, heavy, suffocating people and things in its dense fog. She nodded a slow nod.

'I'll come with you.' Hassan scrambled to his feet. 'I'll find you another pair of sandals.'

'Yes please, Hassan.'

They walked beside the River Euphrates, where the mosquitoes hover in black clouds, buzzing around their sweaty faces. On they walked, past the temples of Shamash and Marduk, making their way amidst the ordinary city folk of Babylon doing normal things in the warm evening sun, eating, drinking, and telling off their children.

At the palace every obstacle was placed in Judith's way. She was told that His Majesty – may he live forever – was taking a bath… in conference with the satraps… at dinner. She had expected this. She was just a girl.

'I'll wait.' Her firm voice surprised her. She stood in the entrance hall and waited. This being dinner time, few people were about. Hassan lowered himself on to the dusty floor a few feet away, watching over her through half-open eyes. She swung him a grateful glance. Daniel would reward him when everything was all right again. *It would be all right, wouldn't it? Soon.*

Still Judith waited. Weary, she sat down on the ledge surrounding the fountain, water occasionally splashing on her robes, but she didn't really care. *It would be all right, wouldn't it?* Some officials appeared, speaking in hushed tones, their footsteps ebbing away, softer and fainter, as they disappeared down the long, stone corridor. *Don't be silly, Judith. Your dad is the most important official in Babylon. Everyone reports to him and he reports only to the king.*

Then suddenly the air bristled. Darius emerged, surrounded by torchbearers and busy courtiers and everyone, including Judith, leapt to their feet. Uncertain of protocol, she remained where she was. But the royal progress was not coming anywhere near her or her fountain and already he was moving towards one of the corridors. She broke into a run. 'Your Majesty, your Majesty.'

He had to stop when she stood right in front of him.

'Oh... um... May you live forever. I'm Daniel's daughter.'

'Er.' He flicked at a minute speck on his purple robe. 'Er.' He was older than she had expected, his face wrinkly and wizened.

'Please, please. Don't do this to him. Please.' She sounded feeble, even to her own ears.

Darius met her gaze for just a moment. 'Um—'

'Please, please. My father, he's a good and honest man. He's served you well. Please, your Majesty, don't—'

'The laws of the Medes and the Persians can never be changed.' The voice of a courtier wearing robes of fine blue cloth filled the hall. The others moved their heads up and down in vigorous nods.

Darius nodded as if recognising what was due to him.

'All he did was pray.' Judith took huge strides to keep pace with him.

'Well, we'll see what his invisible Hebrew God can do to save him now,' said the courtier, swinging open the wide double doors, embossed with jewels. In a moment they would close behind Darius and him, and any hope she might have, disappear.

'He led the Jews out of Egypt,' she cried, running after him, ignoring the sniggers before, behind and beside her. 'He divided the Red Sea.' More titters. 'He brings thunder and lightning.'

'All gods do thunder and lightning.' A courtier who'd been walking backwards and bowing shoved Judith aside. 'Run away, girl.' He hung back as the king and others walked away. 'Take my advice, and get out of Babylon. Fast. His Majesty'll seize all Daniel's property, you know, and his servants... and as for you yourself... Do I need to spell it out?' His tone was not unkind. She recognised him. He had called at their house and eaten at Daniel's table, just ten days ago. Judith and her ladies, sitting in the next room, had heard the two men laughing together in loud guffaws.

With slumped shoulders, she returned to the fountain. Darkness had fallen outside, total blackness except for the torches leading down the palace steps. Total darkness also flooded Judith's heart. She cast another glance towards Hassan. He was still there. *It would be all right, wouldn't it?* 'Don't worry, my little flower,' Daniel always said. 'I'm here.' *But what if Dad wasn't there?*

For the whole night, Judith sat and prayed. Oh yes, she prayed. 'God of Abraham, God of Isaac, hear this daughter of Zion. Free your servant Daniel now. Please, please, Lord. Free Daniel... Daniel... Daniel. Free Daniel, please.' *It would be all right, wouldn't it?*

Guards stood by every doorway, leaning on their weapons and shuffling their feet. From time to time, they cast a cursory glance at the Hebrew girl gazing into the fountain, intent upon clear water tumbling into a boiling pool.

'Oh God of Abraham, please, I beg you, free Daniel now.

Oh Lord, close the lions' mouths. Oh Lord, oh Lord, free Daniel, please.' There she was, breaking the laws of the Medes and the Persians by praying to her Hebrew God all night long, in Darius's own palace. But nobody knew she was doing it. If only Daniel had done it this way.

She must have slept awhile, because she awoke to forks of lightning illuminating the palace courtyard with harsh white daylight for just an instant, then dropping it back into black night. Mighty thunder ripped through Babylon, rumbling, gurgling, slashing the sky, then grey lines of rain beat upon the palace roof like pebbles.

'Praise the Lord,' she mouthed. 'Praise God in his sanctuary.'

A servant, his soggy clothes clinging to every contour of his skinny body, rushed over to Hassan. 'Come on, Miss.' Judith's father's manservant jerked his head towards the main entrance. 'Darius's gone to the lions' den.'

The din upon the roof has ceased, the storm having finished as suddenly as it started.

Dawn broke as they ran back through the city, Judith in sandals struggling to keep up with Hassan's long, barefoot strides. Darius's litter stood by the entrance to the lions' den and also the king himself, still in the purple robe he wore yesterday evening, its sleeves torn as if in mourning. He was pacing around the boulder, which blocked the entrance, barking laconic commands at the soldiers attempting to move it, hardly drawing breath before he started again. 'Come on. Come on. What's the matter with you?'

Judith dared to hope. Or did she?

Darius placed his chubby hands on the sandy rock, as if he himself was about to push, but he couldn't move it. Instead he ran round to the other side, calling, 'Come on. Come on.'

'Come on. Come on,' Judith cried after him.

More servants now had their arms around the rock. When it shifted, gravel crunched underneath it to reveal the mouth of the cave. Judith and Hassan strained to look inside, but they could make out nothing in the blackness below. Then Darius pushed them aside.

They waited. He waited. They all stood there, sneaking glances left and right, their sweat hanging like dew in the arid desert air. Once more, Judith prayed in her head. 'Oh Lord God, bring back Daniel. Daniel, Daniel, Daniel.'

On her last syllable, someone gasped, a loud rasping breath.

A hand. Yes, really, a hand, clawing the mouth of the cave. With Judith's dead mother's ring upon the finger.

'Come on, come on,' shouted Darius again.

Another hand appeared, then Daniel clambered out, in the green, gold-braided mantle, as clean and fresh as when he had put it on yesterday morning.

'Dad. Dad.'

'Judith, Judith, watch where you put your feet. There's lion crap everywhere.'

She wanted to rush over and hug him, claim her father back for herself, but she had to back off as Darius also fell upon him, promising him honours and riches, and the services of His Majesty's own physician.

'I'm fine,' said Daniel, stretching out his arms. 'Judith, you'll never guess what I saw down there. An angel. A real one. In a white frock and with proper wings.

'But Dad, the lions-.'

'Pussycats, my little flower. Just pussycats.'

Kitty's Infernal Machine

I offered to help wash up after afternoon tea, but Cook wouldn't let me. 'Thank you kindly, Thomas Atkins. We can manage for ourselves.'

'Just trying to do my bit, Mrs Pearson,' I said, as I replaced the tea towel on the airer. 'Many hands make light work.'

'I'm sure young Mr Edward's gentleman's gentleman has his own work to do.'

'Indeed I do. And if you'd be so good as to show me where the ironing board is, I'll press his trousers before dinner.'

She flung out a plump arm, bared to the elbow. 'Beside the copper.'

I observed two devices covered by dingy curtains. 'You have two coppers here, I see. 'Pon my word, what a lot of laundry you must have here. Is my master's family so very dirty?'

'Now, now. Remember your place, young man, and that you arrived just this morning.'

'I'll have you know I've been in Mr Edward's service since the end of the war, ma'am, in his rooms in London.' I set up the ironing board with two ear-splitting creaks which drowned out even the sound of the kitchen maid clanking crockery. Out the corner of my eye, I thought I observed her placing cups and saucers into the copper, but, with the evening light streaming from the window, I daresay my eyes deceived me.

'I hear you served with Mr Edward in Flanders,' said Cook.

'Yes.'

'Mentioned in dispatches, he was.' The kitchen maid dropped lye soap into the copper, then lowered the lid. I

28

raised my eyebrows but Cook went on talking. 'Rescued a wounded soldier under enemy fire. Without heed to his own safety. It was all over the *Evening News*.'

'That soldier was me.'

Her eyes widened. 'You?'

I nodded. 'He was the best officer a soldier could hope for. A true gentleman.'

'He is indeed. A crying shame that he came back from the war the way he is.'

'We keep going. One day at a time. Now what are you doing, my dear?' I said this to Kitty, the kitchen maid, who was inserting into the copper a pipe attached to a steam pump on the floor. Cook and the other servants were doing nothing to stop her.

Mrs Pearson called across the kitchen. 'Don't let the water get too hot, Kitty. We can't be washing the patterns off Madam's Royal Worcester again.'

The kitchen maid reached down to the pump and adjusted a valve. *Girls touching machinery?* Water hissed through the pipe, pattering like hail inside the copper, and discharging soapy effluent into a zinc pail. I closed my eyes, wincing for the cups and their thin delicate handles. After a few minutes Kitty leaned forward and raised the lid. Steam billowed, settling on our faces like hot sweat. Giggling like a child, she lifted out a clean side-plate.

'Well done, Kitty,' said Cook. 'Perfectly clean. As always.'

I couldn't help but look inside the copper. 'Gordon Bennett! What...'

'Our washing-up machine, Thomas Atkins. The invention of Kitty, my niece.' Mrs Pearson burst into a grin as she nodded at the kitchen maid who was now removing the rest of the crockery and lining it up on the shelves. 'She doesn't say much but she's good with machinery, our Kitty.

29

Like your Mr Edward. Always tinkering with motor cars, he was.'

During the war he had been handling a different sort of machinery. No washing-up of cups and saucers in the trenches.

'Pull yourself together, dear boy,' shouted my employer's father, Sir Charles Saunders, unaware that I was next door in the dressing room. 'You're twenty-one next month. Key to the door and all that.'

Silence.

'How about that, Edward?'

Silence.

'Your mother and I would like to hold a party for your coming of age. Haven't had a shindig round these parts since before the war.'

More silence.

'Say something, damn you.'

It was a wonder to me that any of the men returning from the trenches managed to put any words into their mouths.

'All I do, Atkins, is tell young men to go over the top and get killed. I can't do it anymore.' This was the last thing Mr Edward said to me, or anyone else.

Sir Charles droned on and on. 'We need to talk about your future. You can't hang around here doing nothing. I bought you the Bentley but you don't use it. It's just sitting there in the old stable block gathering dust.'

This was not true. Kitty used to pop down to the stable block and rub it down. Mrs Pearson and I watched her from the kitchen window. 'I don't know where she gets her mechanical bent. Not from her mama, I'll be bound. My sister was not the practical sort.'

'I don't recall Mrs Pearson's sister,' said Robert the

footman, later as we were cleaning boots. 'Nor does anyone else round here. If you get my meaning.'

I did.

'Kitty grew up here at Waltham Hall. About the same age as Mr Edward, she was. Used to play together as children. With trains and Meccano. Then he went off to Eton and she into service.'

Couldn't Sir Charles see that my poor Mr Edward couldn't cope with a party? Nobs can be so stupid sometimes and I didn't see how I could help. Meanwhile we servants were running around like scalded cats, moving furniture, polishing silver, getting out the Royal Worcester and the Waterford Crystal. Kitty was loading crockery in and out of the washing-up machine all day, but, on the day of the dreaded event, when we were charging around even faster than before, the washing-up machine flooded the kitchen floor. We had been ignoring small leaks for several days. As Kitty mopped up pools of water, her pail filling with grey sludge, the silence amongst us was deafening.

'We can manage without that infernal machine.' Robert kicked the copper. 'The Good Lord gave us hands and washing-up bowls, didn't he?'

I raised my eyes to the ceiling. This evening we had one hundred guests: sherry glasses, four-piece place settings, wine glasses, water glasses, cups and saucers.

Kitty stormed out of the kitchen, her apron over her head, her howls echoing down the corridor.

'She makes a lot of noise for a girl who never speaks. She's not right up in the upper storey.' Robert pointed to his temple.

'I'll trouble you not to speak of Kitty like that in my presence, Robert Bates.' Mrs Pearson thrust her hands on her hips. 'I think you've spoken enough. Haven't you any work to do?' She rounded on me. 'And you, Thomas Atkins. No call for you to stand there gawping.'

I didn't move. 'What are you implying, Robert?' I felt my fists clenching, almost of their own accord, and my chin jutting forward. 'Seeing as my master also cannot speak?'

'Thomas,' Mrs Pearson pushed me towards the kitchen door, 'I'm sure Mr Edward needs you.'

I marched out of the kitchen like the soldier I used to be, attempting to click the heels of my ordinary shoes. I had already laid out Mr Edward's evening apparel in the dressing room, a jacket with velvet lapels, trousers with a narrow stripe at the side, starched tuxedo and white tie. Yet the man himself lay in his bed in the room next door, the eiderdown pulled almost over his head, his eyes shut, and the curtains closed. I braced myself.

'Sir.'

No movement.

'Sir, it's time to get ready.'

He pulled the sheet further over his face.

My platitudes melted into the air of the room. Between us lay no man's land, beyond, barbed wire guarding remembered scenes too painful to revisit.

I drew back the curtains, releasing the sunlight of the English summer. 'We ought to get going.'

He winced at the light.

'Yes. It is a bit bright, isn't it?' I closed the curtain, just a little. *Keep talking, Thomas. All you can do.* 'Lovely afternoon, sir. Lucky the rain's held off.'

He pressed his face back into the pillow.

'Sir.'

He didn't move.

'Sir, it's half past five and it all kicks off at half past six.' No movement.

Had he been younger, I would have dragged off the

32

covers and thrown them down the stairs. I knew about children, being the oldest of eight and I'd given our Ernest this treatment more than once. My fingers itched to touch the eiderdown. But it wouldn't do.

'Come on, sir.' I picked up the hair-brush on the dressing-table and put it down again. 'Let's get this thing over with, shall we?'

Still he didn't move.

'I had a few minutes to read the newspaper this morning. Would you like to hear the news? Mr Lloyd George is still Prime Minister. The Bolsheviks are carrying on with their revolution in Russia. Ah, now... *The Daily Mail* reports that the British dirigible R34 has landed in New York. The first Atlantic crossing by airship.'

He opened his eyes. A glimmer of hope.

'British engineering, eh? You can't beat it.' I wished I'd read the article fully because I couldn't remember anything more.

His gaze drifted down to the eiderdown, following the swirly pattern on the stitching.

Keep talking, Thomas. 'Are you aware, sir, that downstairs in the kitchen... we have a machine which washes-up dishes? It was devised by Kitty, the kitchen maid.'

His eyebrows rose, just a fraction.

'But this afternoon it malfunctioned. Most inconvenient.'

Silence, but he moved, raising his bent elbows above his head as if he were stretching his armpits.

Seizing the moment, I fetched his clothes from the dressing room and got him inside them, then we parted, he to the bathroom, I to lend assistance in the dining room. After we'd finished, I poked my head around the kitchen door, meaning to make my peace with Mrs Pearson, but she was standing by the sink, her plump, freckled arms folded across her ample bosom, her chin tilted upwards, her eyes glinting. 'I can't be doing with this, Thomas Atkins.'

'About Robert, I fear I forgot myself...'

'Never mind Robert Bates. He needs taking down a peg and two from time to time and that's the truth. But look at this. I cannot have Family in the kitchen this evening.'

I looked. My mouth agape, I turned back to her. I looked again. Kitty and my Mr Edward were crouching beside the washing-up machine, an open toolbox beside them. It was like watching two children playing together, catching each other's eyes, nodding and giggling.

'Let them be.' I held my breath. I breathed. 'Let them be.' I held my breath again.

We servants worked around them, as they handed each other tools and pointed to machine parts in silence; even Mrs Pearson returned to the range and her pots. I, though, had to watch the kitchen clock.

Six o'clock, ten past six. Mr Edward and Kitty had cut off the frayed edge of a pipe and refitted it and were now tightening the repaired gasket. 'Sir...' I tapped my watch.

He didn't appear to hear me. He was reaching for the lever which switched on the washing-up machine pump.

Mrs Pearson rushed over, her white apron rustling. 'Begging your pardon, Mr Edward, but I cannot have water all over my kitchen floor again.'

He pressed the lever down anyway.

We waited.

Kitty stood watching, her wet apron clinging to her skirt.

The pump gurgled.

Mr Edward's eyes widened. His body froze.

Then came the familiar hiss in the pipe and the torrent of water beating the base of the copper.

Kitty jumped a little girly jump on the spot.

Scrambling to his feet, my employer and my hero brushed

the dust from the knees of his evening trousers. He held up the sleeve of his dress shirt, stained black with oil and brown with dirty water. 'Atkins…' he said.

He spoke. Yes, he spoke. I wanted to cheer and clap him on the back but he wouldn't like it. 'I'll get you another shirt, sir,' is all I said.

Different Kinds of Gin

April 1922
Potters Bar, London

Today I married your brother, Henry. I hope you understand, Daphne darling. He's alive and he proposed to me. Too much husband-material lies dead in Flanders. I don't fancy becoming an old maid, living off my meagre portion. I have two younger brothers and you know how that goes.

This morning, as we stood in the sitting-room waiting for the wedding carriage, Father offered me Gordon's Gin in one of those old-fashioned pink-flushed glasses my grandmother left him. 'A stiffener.' He met my eye as he said it. Henry has a good job with The Imperial Tea Company and is earning twenty pounds a week. When we arrive in India, we'll have a house. Father's not sentimental and nor am I.

If I'd needed a 'stiffener' it was yesterday evening, when Mother tried to explain the birds and the bees, over weak ladylike tea. I didn't know where to look. Didn't she realise that we had found out about that sort of thing from the older girls in the dormitory? And much more.

What bothers me, my darling Daphne, my best friend for ever, is that this afternoon in church you didn't look at me once. You were sitting on the bridegroom's side, looking beautiful in one of those modern dresses with long beads and a cloche hat, but your lovely hazel eyes were fixed on a point over my head and you didn't speak to me during the reception. I'm worried that you think I've betrayed you. I haven't. We're twenty. We've got to get on with our lives. I hear you're walking out with Jeremy Greatorex.

October1922
Bangalore

We've been in India for almost six months. The sea journey was just ghastly. I spent most of it in our cabin being sick. Henry thought I must be in a family way, but I wasn't and I'm not. I cried in relief when we reached Madras. As we disembarked from the ship, a woman in this scrumptious silk sari hung a garland of jasmine around my neck and Henry's. He got very flummoxed, darting his eyes at me and around the other passengers, as if he'd used the wrong fork at the tea table. I wanted so much to laugh but, dearest Daphne, I had no one to laugh with.

India is busy, busy, busy, so much noise, always somebody shouting and running about, gesticulating. Hawkers, with strings of jewellery hanging from their wrists and carrying wooden models of elephants and other knickknacks, clustered around us like bees in swarm. Everywhere there are beggars: they shuffle along the rough ground on amputated limbs. Some, gripped in motionless despair, hold out their palms in a mockery of stone statues. Others rock backwards and forwards, mumbling mysterious ancient mantras.

We took the train from Madras. Waiting at the station, I thought I was back at home. The British built the Indian railway network, didn't they? So it's just like at home, stations of solid red brick, designed to withstand pelting cold rain and gusty gales from the North Sea, except in India everything's dustier and blacker, and the platforms teeming with people. Indians clamber over the track, then haul each other on to the train, whole families carrying luggage wrapped up in cloths. And they're still doing it ten minutes after the guard's blown his whistle.

Bangalore is bigger than I expected, its skyline dominated by a massive turquoise, pink and yellow Hindu temple, and the more ordinary-looking offices of The Imperial Tea Company. Our house is on the outskirts, a bungalow actually and much like an English house. A few weeks after our arrival, Henry and I were invited to dinner with the managing director and his wife, Mr and Mrs Sparkes. Mr gave us gin and tonic in heavy tumblers, and explained, at huge length, about how the quinine in tonic water prevented malaria and how the British combined tonic with gin to make it palatable. Pompous ass. Mrs, who wore a feather boa and an off-the-shoulder dress, kept telling me, over her long cigarette-holder, 'Anything goes here, my dear. Just anything.'

At first I enjoyed myself hugely, setting up the house and dealing with servants. I've never had servants before, Daphne. It feels so strange getting someone to do things in your own house. But we're all done now and I'm bored. I've never been so bored in my life. Henry is boring. I know he is your brother and all that, but you yourself have said he's boring. The other wives from Imperial Tea are boring. They talk about their children, all the time. I'd never survive Sundays at the club if we weren't drinking gin cocktails. Imagine it, Daphne. Gin with juniper berries, coriander, almonds, orange and lemon peel and all manner of other Indian spices which I can't remember. Honestly, darling, I lurch from one cocktail to the next.

38

Every time I write another letter to you, I think I'll post it this time. But I never do. I've tucked them all away in a drawer in my dressing table. I know you and Henry write and he's told me you're married now. Congratulations. It's fine. Honest injun. It's fine. I will always love you.

July 1924
Shimla

We wives have been packed off to Shimla in the north, to escape the heat in Bangalore. I'm still bored. The only difference is I count down the minutes and hours whilst looking up at the Himalayas. Count down to what? Honestly, Daphne, I don't know. I stroll over to Scandal Point and back every morning, then we girls start on the Beefeaters. The 'scandal' was that a Maharaja eloped with the daughter of the British Viceroy, but nobody knows which Viceroy or whether this happened at all. The women I'm with think it's all terribly romantic and dream of being carried off by Maharajas themselves, but, as you know, I'm different.

April 1927
Bangalore

I have twins, a boy and a girl, Robert and Susan. You may wonder how this happened, Daphne, seeing as when Henry and I got together, nothing happened, not for four years. I didn't know whether the problem was with me or with him. As it's turned out, it was with him. You see, while I was in Shimla, I took matters into my own hands.
Sophronia Sparkes is right; anything goes amongst

39

*our set. Most of the wives go to each other's husbands.
It's all a big joke. Who's going to find out, in England,
I mean? I'm not like that, but needs must. Two pink gins
and I did it. Poor Algernon Parfitt thought I was sweet
on him. I'm more attracted to his wife, Letitia. Petite
and blonde, Daphne dear, with two gnat bites on her
chest. Her beads hang as straight as a plumb line. But
she and I could not transact this particular business
together.*

*Thank you, Algernon. Henry doesn't suspect a
thing. Mother is with us at the moment. She thinks my
little darlings favour Henry. I have to laugh. My
babies are my everything. I'm drinking Guinness
these days. The ayah says it's good for breast-
feeding.*

I can't send you this letter, can I, Daphne?

*September 1938
Bangalore*

*Susie and Bobby set sail from Madras for England
and boarding school a few days ago. Oh Daphne,
watching them go was horrible, like tearing two
limbs from my body. I had to walk away as the boat
steamed from the harbour. They were fine, of course,
excited, talking about 'going home' and 'Auntie
Daphne' meeting them at Southampton. What is
home these days? Our house is silent and boring all
over again. Henry has nothing to say, except what
happens in his office and politics. He tells me the
British will leave India – utterly ridiculous – and that
there'll be another war against Germany. He's lost
weight. Like a waif nowadays. All the unnecessary
worry he puts himself to, I think.*

Letitia Parfitt has nothing to say either, but I don't care. We've better things to do. Oh, Daphne, I have to be honest. It's not just Letitia. Geraldine Hewitt, Jane Wells, even Sophronia Sparkes, are all up for a bit of fun. Our children are in England, our husbands at Imperial Tea offices. Anything goes around here. It doesn't mean anything. We're all so bored. I love you still, even after all these years.

We don't bother with the gin anymore.

August 1946
Madras

I sail for Southampton tomorrow. For the final time. All we British are packing up now. The club is deserted, the big band playing to just two or three couples in the ballroom. The houses where I used to call are empty, and already India is taking over, wooden window frames rotting in the wet and the heat, creeper running up the walls, covering the red brick walls with green. I don't like leaving Henry's grave untended; the last thing I did before departing from Bangalore was to put flowers on it. I did grow to love him in the final days, when he was ill. We used to sit in the garden, watching the bougainvillea and drinking Hatfields (gin and ginger beer to you) slowly, relishing every drop. The doctor said it could do him no further harm. So unfair that he died when I drink so much more than he ever did.

January 1947
Faversham, Kent

I'm writing this letter in your front room, as you prepare breakfast. This one, I will show to you.

41

I didn't know whether I'd be able to cope with visiting you at your house. When I received your letter, I nearly replied to say I had a prior engagement, but you would've suggested an alternative day. I was a bag of nerves. Susie wrote to me reminding me of how jolly Auntie Daphne is and how you visited her and Bobby at school. What did I expect when you opened the door? Mrs Jeremy Greatorex, with a shampoo and set, a ladylike pleated skirt worn with a buttoned-up cardigan. When I look in the mirror, I see one of these too. You invited me only for dinner and I was to take the train back to London, but that never happened, did it?

We poured ourselves Gordon's Gin from a bottle with a red and yellow label, just like the one Father produced before my wedding. We talked and we talked. We moved from the table into the sitting room. We sat together on your settee, Mrs Greatorex's little gilt-rimmed coffee cups with matching spoons on the table in front of us. Your warm body next to mine was enough, your wonderful Daphne smell, your delicious hand on my thigh.

Now it's morning, bitterly cold and your garden's blanketed with fresh snow, virgin-white, as they say. It's still snowing, white blobs falling in diagonal lines upon the already white carpet, soft and deep on the ground. Jeremy's holed up at his club in London and the children are at school. Together at last, my darling Daphne.

Not a Proper Evacuee

4 September 1939.

Auntie Win never says anything nice to me. It's always 'Joyce, take your elbows off the table.' 'Joyce, don't talk with your mouth full.' I don't want to go and live with her in Brimley. I've begged and begged my parents to let me stay with them in London, but they won't.

As the train draws into Brimley Station I try not to burst into tears. My mother reminds me that there is a war on and tells me to pick up my portmanteau. 'You're very lucky to have an auntie living in Essex. You could have been evacuated.' She says this last word in the same tone as she would say 'Nazi'.

When she opens the door to us, Auntie Win's wearing her bright blue district nurse's uniform, 'sensible' black lace-up shoes and wrinkled flesh-coloured stockings. 'Expected you half an hour ago. I have to go out. One of my patients has had a fall. I've made you tea.' She waves her hand at a brown pot with minute white chips on its spout.

Moments later she's swinging her leg over her bicycle and jingling her bell at a dog in the road, leaving us in the kitchen, me counting the faded black and white quarry tiles on the floor and trying to ignore the cabbage smell seeping up my nostrils. My mother smooths her silk dress and brushes the wicker seat of her chair before she sits down.

We're unpacking my suitcase in the little box-room where I am to sleep when we become aware of the hum of conversation and revving of engines in the street below. I step over to the window. 'Buses,' I cry. 'Red London buses.' I pull my mother towards the tiny casement. 'Honestly. Look. It says "London Transport"' on them.' I want to add,

43

'Aren't they splendid? Aren't they spiffing?' but then I think that would be a funny thing to say about buses.

My mother peers over my shoulder and sniffs.

It takes me a moment realise that there's something wrong about these ordinary red Route Masters, lined up behind each other as if in a queue. All the passengers are children. They're tumbling off the landing platforms like ants, clutching gas masks in cardboard boxes and carrying brown paper parcels bundled up with string.

'From the East End, I shouldn't wonder,' says Mum with a sniff.

Proper evacuees, with brown luggage labels tied around their necks. Even though the sun has been shining down upon us all day, I shiver. This war is really happening.

'Joyce, don't stare.' My mother beckons me away with a jerk of her head. 'You be careful around those East Enders. Remember that you live in a nice house in Friern Barnet. And that your father's the manager at the bank.'

'Yes, Mummy.'

'What's the time?' My mother raises her wrist to her nose, and squints at her tiny silver-framed watch. She says glasses don't suit her. Picking up her handbag, she reaches over to kiss my cheek. 'I'd better take the four thirty-two, darling. Daddy and I are going out to dinner tonight. You'll be all right until Auntie Win comes home, won't you?

I gulp in a short breath. I want to scream, 'Please don't,' and 'Please, please, please... take me home,' but I'm twelve. I force a smile. Wartime spirit and all that.

I continue to watch the buses after she's left. I wonder if I could stow away under one of the seats and travel back to London, and I carry on thinking about this long after the drivers have clambered back into their cabs and driven off, around the corner and out of sight. For several minutes I hear their clattering engines, then nothing, only the shopkeeper over the road snapping up his blind. If only I were fourteen. Fourteen-year-olds are allowed to stay in London, my wonderful, wonderful London. If only we had relatives in America, like my friend, Eileen. She's sailing on the Queen Mary tomorrow. Lucky thing. Daddy's suggested I keep this diary.

6 September 1939

I've started at Brimley Grammar School for Girls. The buildings are old, with long corridors painted grass green and mustard yellow, a tiny yard where we're supposed to spend break and no hockey pitches or tennis courts. There are so many of us in the form room that some pupils have to share a desk, or even kneel on the floor. The village girls have bagged all the places on one side of the room and the evacuees, from Deptford, the other side. I sit at a single desk at the middle, in front of a pillar and pipes which gurgle like someone being sick.

When Miss Clough asks us to introduce ourselves, I'm last. 'Joyce Harper, Miss,' I say. 'From Friern Barnet Ladies' Academy.'

Someone behind me sniggers.

5 October 1939

Everyone at school keeps calling me 'Friern Barnet'. The Deptford girls started it. They say I talk posh and I'm stuck up. I don't and I'm not.

I've just spoken to Mummy from the telephone box down the road. I asked her about coming home, just for a weekend, but she won't let me. It's not fair. The Germans haven't dropped any bombs in London. I didn't tell her anything about school, of course. She's doing war work, knitting for the WRVS, and Daddy's an air raid warden.

Auntie Win's listening to 'The News' on the wireless when I get back, men talking about the war, very serious. Mummy says the BBC make them wear evening dress when they're on air. Then suddenly the announcer's voice fades out and that horrid Lord Haw-Haw comes on. Nobody knows who he is, or even if he's one person or several, although his – or their – accent is British.

After his broadcast has finished I feel like icy water is running through my veins. Auntie Win makes more cocoa. She makes good cocoa. We don't talk about Lord Haw-Haw. We don't talk much at all. She reads the newspaper and I do my homework.

26 October 1939

They're calling me names again. They stopped for a few days and now they've restarted. It's my own fault, I suppose. I mentioned my old school again during algebra. I'm not a tell-tale, but I did speak to Miss Clough this morning and she was jolly decent. This afternoon she sent me out of class with a message for the headmistress's secretary, and, when I returned, she was saying to the class, 'We must just call her just "Joyce". That's her name.'

31 October 1939

Nothing goes right for me.

It's all over the papers that Lord Haw-Haw's name is 'William Joyce'. The other girls are following me around, chanting, 'Jairmany calling, Joyce... Jairmany calling, Joyce.' I hate them all. The rotten thing is that, when Marjorie and Tilly came over at break this morning, I thought they want to be friends and I smiled at them, but immediately they started. 'Jairmany calling, Jairmany calling.' I hate them. I hate them all so much.

That afternoon, when I return from school, Auntie Win's telling me off about leaving clothes on my bedroom floor. 'A place for everything and everything in its place.' She says this all the time.

I've had enough. I'll tidy my bedroom, all right. I'll tidy it so she won't know I've ever been here.

I lug my suitcase downstairs, bumping it over each step and making a lot of noise, but fortunately Auntie Win's using the outside lavatory and doesn't hear. I'm afraid of damaging the case, or the catch bursting open, but it's all right. I slip out the front door. I've 5s 2d in my purse. That's going to be enough, surely. I trundle down the street, dragging my heavy luggage behind me. I never realised how uneven the Brimley pavement is, and the handles on my case are really hurting my hands. I have to keep swapping from left to right, but, like the war poster says, I carry on. Into the station booking office at last, I ask for a single to Liverpool Street. Ah, the music of those words.

'Six shillings,' says the booking clerk.

I empty the contents of my purse on to the counter, pushing my coins towards him, shillings, sixpences, threepenny bits, pennies, halfpennies and farthings. I watch the lines on his face and his sprouting eyebrows. He's smiling. I'm sure he's a nice man. He's got to be a nice man. No, he's not.

He's shaking his head. 'Six shillings, Miss.'

'Pleeaase.'

'Six shillings to you. Same as everybody else.' Calling 'Yes?' over my head to the soldier in uniform behind me, he shoves my coins back across the wooden counter.

The Deptford girls – the real evacuees – would have argued the toss. *C'monnn Misterrrr. Gimmee.*

I'm Joyce, from Friern Barnet. And still in Brimley.

I trudge back through the village, past the Co-op, the

church, my school, and all the other horrible dreary buildings. Autumn is here now. Dusk is falling and, with the blackout, it goes dark fast. Only the fish and chip shop gives out a faint blue glow.

Ten minutes later I'm staring at the leaded fanlight over Auntie Win's porch, papered over as required by the War Office. I lift my hand to knock then let it drop. I'll do it. In a minute.

A piercing sound like splitting wood has me staggering backwards. The front door, swollen with October damp, rips open. My aunt, a yellow cardigan over her blue nurse's dress, hovers in the doorway, her hand on the lintel. Her complexion, never beautiful like my mother's, is drained of any colour, except for prominent brown freckles and pink broken veins.

'Joyce. Thank God.' She grabs my wrist and yanks me inside.

'I...'

'Your mother... What could I have said to your mother?' She sees my suitcase. She cannot tear her eyes away from it.

'I'll... I'll take it upstairs.' I'm speaking so low I can hardly hear myself.

'I'll make some cocoa.'

My hands sore, and striped red and white by my suitcase handle, I take my belongings back to my room. She calls up to me three times, even though I'm quick, staying upstairs only to remove my outdoor shoes, which she doesn't allow me to wear in her house. I go downstairs and I sit at the kitchen table, once more counting the black and white quarry tiles, aware of her moving about and making cocoa, but not daring to look at her. 'I'm afraid you do have to stay here, Joyce,' says Auntie Win, as she hands my cup to me.

'I know.' I take a gulp of steaming chocolate froth. It scalds my throat. 'The war.'

48

She sips her own, swallowing loudly. Usually she's a tea person. 'Your bedroom... it wasn't too untidy. I shouldn't have said anything. I'm sorry.'

What did she just say? I shuffle in my seat.

'I'm a nurse. I'm afraid I expect everything to look like a hospital.'

'I'll make it all tidy when I put it everything back,' I say. Grown-ups don't apologise to children. It's not the proper thing.

'Thank you.' She sits back in her chair, sliding forwards as if she's lying on it. 'How are things at school?'

'All right.'

'Really? Unless girls have changed a lot since my day, they can be absolutely horrible.'

I want to cry, but not in front of Auntie Win. I rush upstairs to my room and she doesn't call me, but I come back down after a minute or two anyway because I want my cocoa and we just sit, either side of the table. When I do talk, she doesn't put her arm around me and stroke my hair like Mummy would, but she does listen and she nods a lot. She already knew, of course. People talk in villages.

'Pity you mentioned the "Ladies Academy" bit,' she says at last.

'It's what my school's called.'

She raises her eyebrows.

'Really, Auntie Win, I'm not stuck up.'

'I know, but think about how it sounds to other people.' She grabs her handbag. 'With all this going on, I haven't put tea on. Let's buy fish and chips. We'll sort out those girls. You see.'

We've been standing waiting outside the chip shop for a while when Marjorie (from Brimley) and Tilly (from Deptford) join the queue. 'Those two're in my form,' I say to Auntie Win.

49

'Say hello then.'

I turn away. 'They're horrid.'

'They're waving to you.'

I shake my head.

'Come on, Joyce. Be friendly. Wave back.'

I don't want to, but I do, because Auntie Win's glaring at me.

'And smile.'

I force my mouth into a tight sort of grin.

An icy wind, straight off the North Sea, whips through my Friern Barnet coat. Tilly says it's cold in Brimley because the wind blows from Germany. Tilly can be all right sometimes. When I get my meal, wrapped up in *The Daily Sketch*, I clasp it to my chest like a hot water bottle. 'Mummy doesn't let me eat in the street, but would it be all right if I had a few chips?'

Auntie Win is already unravelling her bundle of newsprint. 'Mum,' she says. 'Mum.'

I frown. 'Mummy wouldn't like being called Mum.'

'Call her what you like... in Friern Barnet... and don't eat in the streets... in Friern Barnet. But this is Brimley and I'm Auntie Win.'

'You and she don't get along, do you?'

'Of course we do,' my aunt says almost before my words are out. She bites off a large piece of fish and chews it slowly. She nudges me as we're about to pass Marjorie and Tilly. 'Offer them some chips.'

My arm locks by my side.

'Go on.'

I thrust my bag in front of them. 'Er... would you like a chip.'

Tilly looks at Marjorie, at Auntie Win, at me, at Auntie Win again, then giggles as she grabs two. 'Watcha,' she says. Her way of saying 'thank you,' I think.

'Watcha' says Marjorie, taking one. Marjorie copies everything Tilly says.

'Well done,' says Auntie Win as we cross the road. 'Now, in future, don't let them, or any of the other girls, see that they upset you.'

We're just finishing our meal when two figures come hurtling up the street, shouting, 'Joyce, Joyce!'

'Have a chip, Joyce.' Tilly holds out her portion.

'Would you care for a chip, Nurse Carter?' asks Marjorie. She stares up at her. 'You looked after my grandma last year, when she had her stroke, didn't you?'

Auntie Win nods. 'Yes, of course. How's Grandma now?'

'Very well, thank you,' says Marjorie. 'Actually, not really.'

'I'll drop by tomorrow, Marjorie.'

'You can come around with us at break tomorrow, if you want, Joyce,' says Tilly through chewed potato. She swings on her heel to face Marjorie. 'Can't she, Marge?'

'Do you think she means it, Auntie Win?' I say as we walk home.

'Only one way to find out.'

Burnt Down

Susan saw The Thing as they entered the park. For a few scary moments, she couldn't take her eyes off it. Then she turned away and she couldn't look at it again.

Two little dogs were chasing each other around in circles, barking yaps of excitement. A couple lay on the grass, arms around each other's shoulders, listening to pop music on their transistor, to a song about a 'Mrs Robinson' who made something called cup-cakes. Buses rumbled in the distance, carrying the secondary school children back home for an evening of tea, homework and television. Pale yellow primroses and blue forget-me-nots spread themselves over the flowerbeds, bursting with the hope of spring and of summer fast approaching.

As if the dark and strange Thing wasn't there.

She could hear the happy squeals and splashing of children playing in the outdoor pool. All week Susan had begged to come here to Abbey Park, even though May had not yet passed.

Yet The Thing's blackness loomed over her like a bully's fist, even now she had her back to it. The sun was shining, but a clammy coldness seeped through the little gaps between the stitches in her woolly cardigan.

'Burnt down, two weeks ago,' said Grandma, shielding her eyes from the sun with her hand to get a better view.

Burnt down. Susan's shiver jolted against her ribs, stirred around in her tummy, and moved down her legs to her knee-length socks and across the bar of her Start-Rite shoes.

'Pity,' said Grandma. 'They made a lovely cup of tea in that café and, last time we came, that nice waitress gave you three scoops of strawberry ice cream even though I'd only paid for two.'

In a tall green bevelled glass, with a frilly white doily underneath, the ice cream as pink as her party frock, Susan could still taste the sweetness of her treat. She shivered again.

Her grandmother frowned. 'I'm not letting you go in the pool today, Susan. Too cold and you're not looking quite right.'

She didn't object.

'We'll go around the ruins of the Abbey.'

The Abbey held no terrors for her, even though her teacher, Miss Bailey, had told her class a legend about a phantom who raced through the park in a coach and horses and back to her old home in the Abbey. Susan didn't know what a phantom was and the word didn't sound frightening when Miss Bailey said it. She skipped along the low stone Abbey walls, holding out her arms to balance.

'Better be off home now,' said Grandma. 'Getting on for teatime.'

Susan caught a glimpse of The Thing's blackness, from the corner of her eye as they exited the park. It seemed to leap out at her even though she was trying so hard not to see it.

Her grandmother squeezed her fingers. 'I do believe you're fretting yourself about that phantom. It's just a story, Susan. Don't you worry yourself about it.'

Susan's mother was feeding the baby when they arrived home. Stroking little Janey's head, warm, pink and velvety soft, as she glugged at the breast, Susan felt better. The Thing was a long way away now and Grandma said she didn't want to return to Abbey Park seeing as there was nowhere to buy a cup of tea.

Susan was all right until Mummy switched off the light at bedtime, but in the gathering dusk The Thing loomed in front of her, a dense blackened shell, jagged roof timbers protruding into the sky, and red tiles, heaped like shingle against the gable. She pressed her face into her pillow but, whatever she did, she couldn't make it go away. She could see the fire, flames roaring and crackling, billowing around her tall green bevelled glass. Had the pink dregs of her ice cream hissed in the bottom of the dish as they burned?

But—

'You're a big girl now,' Grandma had said, as she had said goodbye that afternoon. 'Make sure you help Mummy.'

Susan turned over in bed. Yes, she was a big girl. She was eight.

In time, the Council demolished the burnt-down shell and in its place built a cafeteria. Teas were served in plastic cups with the teabags left in the bottom. No silver dishes now, ice creams were passed through the servery hatch in wrappings which stuck to the ice cream itself and had to be peeled off shred by shred. There were also cup-cakes in crinkly paper cases.

Grandma did not approve, but any tea was better than no tea.

Susan did not like it either. She was relieved that the burnt-down Thing was no longer there to see, but it seemed wrong for there to be another eatery on the same spot. As if the old café's feelings were being hurt.

The new cafeteria closed in winter, the Council's understanding of this season being that it started on 1 September. Susan and Grandma had not realised this, when they trundled up the hill where it stood, with Janey in her pushchair, on 2 September. The serving hatch was boarded up with wooden shutters and the bin outside, not yet emptied, contained plastic cups, ice cream wrappers and paper cup-cake cases.

Out of breath, Grandma applied the pushchair brakes and reached in her handbag for her packet of cigarettes and her matches.

Susan watched the small flame flicker at the end of the matchstick, and the short-lived red glow of tobacco at the end of Grandma's Woodbines. All the grown-ups in her family smoked and, she assumed, she would too one day. A dropped cigarette had caused the fire at the – old – café, so Mummy had told Daddy. Susan ran through the scene in her mind, as she had done so many times from her bed. A little spark would catch a bit of paper. It would crackle as it burned, with yellow flames which would catch one of the white linen tablecloths. Higher and higher the fire would burn, leaping towards the wooden window frames of the building...

Janey, desperate to get out and play, was arching her back and straining against the straps of her wheeled restraint. Grandma attempted to release her but the fastenings were awkward. Janey threw back her head and whinged.

Susan put her hand inside her grandmother's bag, and felt the objects inside, a purse, a house key, a lipstick... a matchbox. She knew she shouldn't, but she did it anyway. Sneaking a furtive glance at her grandmother's back, she pulled out the matchbox and ran her finger over its rough edge, relishing its grown-up fragrance.

The fierce flame which leapt from it when she pulled the match against the edge of the box was scary. And hot, really hot, burning her fingers. Without thinking, she tossed it into the waste bin.

The flame flickered, working its way down the thin wooden matchstick, yellow turning darker and darker red then dwindling... Suddenly, it caught a lolly wrapper. Yellow again and with more vigour, it edged up the bin. The girl looked on, her eyes widening, her mouth opening in a round O. So, this was how it had looked before.

A hot shimmer zapped through her spine. A cold shiver clutched her stomach at the same time. *Oh no, oh no, oh no.* She clenched her teeth as if to hold the fire down. *What have I done?*

'Come along, love,' said Grandma, gathering little Janey under her arm. 'No point in staying here if you can't get a cup of tea.' She held out an opened palm. 'And it's coming on to rain. Come on, loves.'

Grandma, tea, rain and everything ordinary. Averting her eyes from this terrible new Thing which she had caused herself, Susan concentrated hard on watching her grandmother put her little sister back into the pushchair... refasten the reins... and release the brakes at last. It was raining heavily now.

'Come on,' said Grandma again.

Susan had to take a last look at the new Thing. She braced herself for a roaring inferno, white flames leaning and stretching towards the main building. But... but... there was nothing, except smouldering smoke. She rushed over to the bin, peering inside to make sure.

'Susan.' Grandma stretched out her hand. 'Come on.'

That night, when the lights were turned off, The Thing had gone from Susan's bedroom wall.

Anna the Dissident

September 1979

The first time Anna heard the D word used against her was on the day of the Holy Father's visit to Krakow. After attending open air Mass outside the Wawel Cathedral, she and several thousand others were walking back to ordinary life. Passing historic buildings blackened by soot from the local steelworks and clutching her tiny red and white Polish flag, Anna was too old to be as excited as the younger ones were but she was content.

She was turning into the street where she'd parked when she spotted a Westerner hovering beside her red Polski Fiat. 'Bob Heine. South California Times, ma'am.' He held up a small card she was unable to read without her glasses.

She waved both her hands in front of her. 'No, no. Not speak,' she said in English, a language she knew a little. Pushing him aside she shoved her car key into the door lock. As usual it jammed and she was expecting to have to make several painful twists of her arthritic wrists in order to get back into her car.

'Allow me.' It yielded to him at once. 'So, ma'am, how will the Pope's visit affect morale amongst Polish dissidents like yourself?'

'Dissident? No dissident.'

'You're the wife of Jerzy Krol.'

'Widow.' She stared ahead, at the marks left by flies on the windscreen. 'He died. In prison. In 1968. You know nothing.' The car started first time for once, farting automotive disgust from its exhaust. 'How dare he, Jerzy?' she cried as she headed out of the city towards the Tatra Mountains. 'We're radicals... Catholics... Poles.'

September 1980

Anna inched out her front door, scanning the street for the usual black car with one leather-jacketed man sitting inside. That evening there was none. 'Too busy running after *Solidarnosc* nowadays. Can't waste time on an old woman like me,' she said to herself, as she panted up the mountain and into the forest clearing, where she and her 'group' met weekly to rant about the government, and at each other, unseen and unheard.

Walking back afterwards she became aware of Roman standing by the front porch and looking up the road, shielding his face against the reddening sun with his palm. 'Mother?'

She raised her arms then let them drop against her sides. 'Here I am.'

'*Dobry?*' He affected to adjust the stack of honey pots by the gate.

'Yes.' She nodded at the handwritten sign resting on the top jar advertising 'All Polish Honey for Sale'. 'Is this true, *moj drogi?* Maybe our bees occasionally fly over the border into Czechoslovakia?'

He studied her face.

She biffed him on the shoulder. 'Of course they wouldn't. Our bees, my son, are proud to be *Polski*.'

Only then did his face crease into a faint grin. Roman's sense of humour was undeveloped.

'I'm going away for a few days, Roman. In the car.'

'Where?'

'Away.'

'Mother...

Their blue grey eyes clashed like jousting swords. 'To the coast.'

'Bit cold for swimming in the Baltic.'

She held her glare. 'Before I go, could you carry that old typewriter downstairs and put it on the back seat? It takes up too much space in my room.'

He sneaked a sidelong glance towards his wife, Julia, who was lifting carrots from the vegetable patch. 'You're going to Gdansk, aren't you?' he said.

Anna did not reply.

'*Solidarnosc*. That's it, isn't it?'

'Father would've been there. With the strikers at the Gdansk Shipyard last month.'

'*Puh*. He would've got himself arrested, while Walesa hobnobbed with the government.' Jerzy had been thrown into prison in August 1968 as Soviet tanks rolled into Czechoslovakia to crush the Prague Spring, a movement with which he had had no involvement. The following winter he had succumbed to pneumonia in a freezing cell.

'Did you know about those strikes beforehand?' Roman asked her.

'No.' She would've loved to have answered yes.

'*Solidarnosc's* appealing for office equipment.'

Her eyes widened.

'Like everyone else around here, I listen to overseas radio stations. *Solidarnosc* require many many things, printing presses, copiers – and typewriters, Mother – which they cannot buy without being registered with the government.'

'Don't believe everything you hear from overseas radio, Roman, although…' She nodded vigorously several times. 'You are correct in this instance.'

'Why aren't the young men in your group doing this?'

'I volunteered.'

'I wish you wouldn't.'

'You forget, Roman, that I'm your mother and you're my son. Not the other way round. Bring the typewriter to my car, please. I'm going inside now.'

'Wait…'

Her bladder required frequent and urgent attention, having been weakened thirty-seven years ago in a dingy room in Krakow when she had given birth to him, her one and only child. From her window she'd watched the Nazis corralling the Jews along the street, poor women in headscarves, clattering pots and pans behind them, dark-eyed children clutching their mothers' skirts. Assaulted by pain every few minutes, Anna wondered when the Germans would come for her and the other Poles who had tried to help their Hebrew friends. After the birth, when she had stopped screaming, the city was silent, except for the rustling of her stale sheets.

After the war Jerzy said, 'Now we have peace, and a Socialist government, things'll improve.'

He was wrong. They formed the group in nineteen forty nine.

September 1980 (still)

It amused Anna that nowadays her son wore a red and white *Solidarnosc* badge on his jacket. He'd never involved himself in her and Jerzy's activities; even as a child, he knew where not to look, what questions not to ask. After a lot of grumbling and procrastination, Roman did carry the heavy typewriter downstairs and fitted it between the front and back seats of Anna's Polski Fiat. She set off immediately afterwards, her little car whining its protest as she drove along steep mountain roads, past chalets with corrugated-iron roofs dipping to the ground and one tethered cow grazing on the front verge. White posters of the Polish Pope, John Paul II, smiled from every window, alongside darker images of the Black Madonna of Jasna Gora. This was her Poland, Jerzy's Poland.

That night Anna tried to sleep in her car, scrunched up into a tight foetal position, with her head pressing against the door handle. In the darkest hours before dawn, she dozed, dreaming of arriving at *Solidarnosc's* headquarters, and finding typewriters on every desk, sometimes two or three. In the kinder light of morning, she drank water from her bottle, pleasantly chilled by the night air.

Gdansk was bigger than she anticipated, a city of towering, dun-coloured apartment blocks, every window-pane displaying a red and white *Solidarnosc* sticker, every lamppost, every road sign. 'Look, Jerzy,' she cried. 'Oh Jerzy, just look.'

'The Hotel Morski is on the road to Sopot,' said the group member who knew somebody who knew somebody who'd taken part in the Shipyard Strikes. 'You can't miss it.' She could.

So much traffic, worse than Krakow. A red and white tram, which wouldn't – and mechanically couldn't – stop for anyone came hurtling down its track within centimetres of Anna's wing mirror. Drivers honked their horns when she slowed to consult road signs which attempted to direct her to northern towns she'd never heard of. So many people and not ordinary Polish people. These strange human beings wore Western clothes, took long confident strides and held clipboards and notebooks. Whenever she stopped at traffic lights, they were walking behind... also in front... and beside her little Polski Fiat.

Anna caught a glance of the Shipyard crane on the skyline, its jib bent like a bird's broken wing, but, as when encountering someone famous in the street, she knew she mustn't stare. Round and round she went, through the same junctions, past the same shops and the same woman in a flowery housecoat, smoking outside a hair salon. When Anna eventually pulled up beside her, the hairdresser waved her cigarette towards the seafront, before Anna had even spoken. Had this woman been one of those who had stood outside the Shipyard, hour after hour, day after day, supporting her husband or son? Anna drove on, down strange roads, leading to more roads, and yet another road. The traffic was slowing again, and drivers leaning out of their open windows to gawp. Were they weighing up the motor vehicles in the showroom she was travelling alongside? No. A dingy sign over the adjacent doorway whispered 'Hotel Morski'.

'I've found it, Jerzy.' Several floors up, a handwritten banner strung across several casements screamed 'SOLIDARNOSC'.

But how was she supposed to get in? She could see the banners hanging over the upper storeys but the showroom was at street level and she could see no obvious entrance or a doorway marked *Solidarnosc*.

Demonstrators were marching towards her, their rumbling chanting swelling in volume and intensity. Another group – steelworkers according to the boards they held – milled about a speaker whose voice boomed distorted words through a loud-hailer. Long-haired teenagers, who should be in school, stuck flyers everywhere, including on Anna's windscreen. She stretched her arm out of her window to remove the flapping piece of paper, but couldn't quite reach. The boy who'd put it there waved and grinned.

With difficulty she manoeuvred herself into a roadside parking space. Out of habit Anna cowered behind her steering wheel, watching for uniformed police and their plain clothes colleagues. The silence when she switched off the ignition was deafening.

A ginger-haired young woman wearing a *Solidarnosc* T-shirt was speaking very fast and in English, at a gaggle of western journalists holding fur-covered microphones.

'Press conference. One hour.' She held up her flat palm. 'No questions now.'

'And you are...' they asked.

'Marya Weiclawski, *Solidarnosc* spokeswoman.'

Anna shook her head. 'Don't give out your full name, you stupid girl.' She didn't know even the group members' surnames.

The reporters dispersed, brushing past her vehicle, one of them knocking against it. 'Sorry,' he said. Anna recognised Bob Heine of the *South California Times* but he wasn't bothering her now the big players were out.

The teenagers stuck another flyer under her windscreen. The demonstrators were heaving towards her in a wave, chanting '*Solidarnosc, Solidarnosc.*' Anna drew in her breath and held it. Her lungs filled to bursting point. There was not enough air in her small car. What little there was, she had used up over two days. She had to get out. Anywhere. Anyhow. She didn't care about the typewriter anymore.

Grabbing her handbag, she dragged her stiff legs out on to the pavement. More protesters approached, forcing her against the side of her Polski Fiat, the coldness of its red metal penetrating through her thin skirt. Once again she struggled to lock the door. Tears brimmed up in her eyes on seeing Roman's sweater on the back seat. She was so far away, from him and everything familiar. *No, no, she mustn't cry now.*

Swallowing hard, she crossed the street. Then she stopped. She had no idea where she was going in this strange city. She swivelled on her heels. *No... no.* The car! She must get back into her little Polski Fiat and Roman's jumper and drive out of this weird place and back home.

But, actually, she did care about the typewriter. She cared very much. The typewriter was her reason for being here.

A sharp wind whipped into Anna's favourite cardigan,

forcing it open and thrusting its icy blast through the thin fabric of her old blouse. The *Solidarnosc* spokeswoman was striding along the pavement, her arms crossed over her chest against the cold. Anna spoke aloud. 'She knows where she's going, Jerzy. She'll know the way in, Jerzy… Stop. Stop. *Panna*… stop.'

Anna's voice dissolved into the general hubbub, *Solidarnosc* noise, not hers.

'Panna… Marya.' Anna didn't like calling strangers by their first names. It was not how her generation did things.

But the *Solidarnosc* girl halted her stop. 'Yes?' she said, her eyes not lifting from her clipboard.

'I've got a typewriter. For *Solidarnosc*.' Anna spoke in a whisper, even though everyone else was shouting.

'Thank you,' she replied, still not looking up.

'If *Solidarnosc* still wants typewriters…' Her dream of last night returned in all its vividness.

'Of course.'

'*Aj, dobry, dobry*.' The relief drained Anna's last drop of energy. 'It's in my car. You… I mean… *Solidarnosc'll*… have to get it out. It's too heavy for me.' She longed to sit down, but nowhere was there a seat or bench.

'Yes. Er… sure.' Marya turned, about to go, then she swung around. '*Pani*, are you all right?

Anna drew herself up. 'I'm fine.' She raised her eyebrows. 'So, you're going to arrange for someone to fetch the typewriter?'

'Yes, yes. I'll get one of the Shipyard workers. They're used to lifting heavy stuff.'

As she re-crossed the road to wait by her car, the words 'Shipyard worker' sang in Anna's brain. Now she had time to look, at every slogan, every chant, every banner. And to drink it all in. This was what she had come for. As a dissident.

The Witch

She's been wagging her bony finger in his face for twenty minutes, telling him what to do. She's still talking when our president – the one I'm sworn to protect with my life – is stepping across the balcony towards the rack of microphones fixed to the railings. They're all there: BBC, CNN, RTE, even our own national television station.

I await the customary roar of applause. But none comes.

Sss sss.

He leans forward. He taps one of the wired furry devices in front of him. 'Al-oo?

Sss sss.

I glance at Constantin, two metres in height and almost as broad. He looks back at me, his dark eyes saying nothing as usual. I feel in my pocket for my revolver and I observe him doing the same. We thought we had the crowd fixed, even though I did have to threaten some workers with the sack if they didn't get themselves into Palace Square today. They're all there, at the front where I told them to be, holding up the banners of him and her which we supplied them with. But even with the darkest threats, I cannot fill the whole Square.

'Al-oo?' I used to find it endearing how the president's mouth forms into a rectangle as he speaks.

Sss sss.

He turns to me. 'What… What are they saying?'

I don't answer. Nor does Constantin. We played our part in putting down the demonstrations in the town which sounds like sss only a few weeks ago.

He raises his hand and waves. 'Al-oo. Al-oo.' He lifts his hand higher and waves again, a stiff, unnatural movement, like an amateur actor in a role to which he's unsuited, even after all these years in office.

Sss… sss.

'Comrades… comrades… stay quiet.'

The noise level swells.

It's never before occurred to me how slight he is, an ordinary little man in a black coat, a checked scarf tucked around his throat, a Russian bearskin perched upon his thinning grey hair. Or are we all, even the solid bulk that is Constantin, dwarfed and mocked by the classical columns of the palace, ten, fifteen, twenty times his height and mine?

With the slightest curl of her forefinger, she beckons him back to the doorway where she's standing. He goes to her at once, as always. They say she's a world-famous chemist, but – *puh* – she with that thin pointed chin and steel-grey wispy hair, her powers come from no laboratory.

Constantin steeples his fingers behind his back, into the shape of a conical hat. Our private joke.

'Talk to them. Talk to them.' She pushes him forward. I take note of her glossy nylon tights, almost certainly purchased from the west. *Puh. Puh.* My wife, Veronika, has only old, scratchy things, with sewn-up holes.

He talks, leaning forward over the balustrade, gesturing with his hand and clenching his fist. He promises increases in living standards, in salaries and allowances for children.

She's clapping. Constantin and I are clapping too, on autopilot, but down in the street below, in that groaning, heaving mass of humanity, there is no echo. Anger and hatred rise from the crowd like stale fart and hang like a dense blanket of smog, the desperate anger of those who cannot fill their bellies, cannot get warm in the depths of our winter and cannot buy even the meanest Christmas presents for their families. Then they do clap, a slow and rhythmic clap weighed down with derision.

'Sir… the helicopter. On the roof. Next door.' Why do I address him as 'Sir'?

His fist clenched and half-raised, he shakes his head.

The witch comes forward, nudging him aside. 'Comrades... comrades... what's wrong with you?' She swings around and glares at him. 'The Palace. Remind these ungrateful... peasants... that we're building them the Palace.'

'Er... We're building you a palace. A... people's... palace.'

The mirth of the people ricochets off the hard marble walls and around the Square.

Hunger grinds in my belly. Every moment of the day, I dream of crispy roast tripe. 'The helicopter,' I say again. I haven't eaten meat for several weeks.

He nods.

We scuttle off the balcony and back into the Palace, over mosaic floors and along seemingly endless bare-walled corridors, which we will never see again, down wide and curving staircases of veined cream marble. We dare not trust the lifts. Then out and up-up-up again, through the many floors of the adjacent Communist Party offices. He huffs and puffs and clutches his chest, but demonic powers propel her thin spindly legs upwards.

Vlad has the helicopter engine running on the roof, a noisy beast, whirring and clattering, like our country's factories used to. As we scramble aboard, our president says, 'Take us away. We have friends.'

I smirk. 'Who?

He doesn't reply.

'Perhaps Lech Walesa, now democratically-elected president of Poland? He'll be so very pleased to see you. Or Vaclav Havel in Czechoslovakia?'

Without turning to face her, I feel her piggy eyes boring into me and her evil washing over me like a glacial wave. 'Remember who you're talking to. I can make things very difficult for you... and your wife. Veronika, isn't it?' She calls to Vlad, strapping himself into the cockpit. 'Take us to Baghdad. To Saddam Hussein.'

'No need to bother Saddam,' I say, 'we've got everything ready for you.'

After we've shot them, we show photographs of their bodies on television. Our fellow countrymen need to know – beyond doubt – that the witch and her familiar are dead.

Tomatoes and Their Part in Brexit

I'm standing by the tomato counter in Waitrose. Cherry tomatoes, plum tomatoes, beef tomatoes, organic tomatoes, tomatoes in packets, loose tomatoes, every sort of round lump in every size and every possible shade of red. *Which ones did Vincent say he liked?*

The overhead lights, reflected in their glistening scarlet skins, blink at me. *Come on. Don't dither, Julie. Pick me. Me, me, me.* In the old days, I could do my supermarket shop in ten minutes. All around me, I hear the bleep-bleep of handheld scanners, of other customers making decisions, as I used to be able to. Behind me, a husband and wife discuss what to eat tonight and how they were going tomorrow to his sister who always serves shepherd's pie – such a couple-y conversation. I want to tap them on the shoulder and tell them that, for the first time in decades, I have a partner. *Yes, I know I look too old. I retired last year.*

Vincent gave me a lift in this afternoon. He's so kind, stopping right in front of the main door at Waitrose, because it's raining. He didn't seem to notice that the queue of cars waiting behind him. He's gone to visit his mother. A man *should* spend time with his mother. It's only right. And he lived under her roof all his life, until he came to be with me three weeks ago. And you know the best thing about it? He went to Mother's this morning by himself. *Whoops. Shouldn't be uncharitable.*

'Heritage' tomatoes. That was what he said he liked. I saw them in Waitrose a little while ago, but where are they now? A woman in tight jeans stretches across me to grab a packet marked 'reduced', muttering 'Sorry' without looking up. *Oh, there they are, the heritage tomatoes, right at the back at the top.* Being vertically challenged, I need to ask tight jeans woman to reach them for me. She does it with a watery smile.

I get chatting to an elderly couple as I'm waiting for the checkout. I never used to strike up conversations with strangers but I find myself doing it all the time these days. When I mention that Vincent's an artist, they tell me that their daughter works in graphic design and has 'a very good job' building images for websites. 'Vincent's a painter,' I say. 'Abstracts. He tries to explain it all to me but... well, I'm not artistic. He says the public isn't ready for his work yet. But Cavenham Gallery have taken a couple of his canvasses. Do you know the Cavenham Gallery?... Yes, of course. You've got to go. Nice talking to you.'

On the way home in the car, it seems that every house, every farm and every field is displaying a red *Leave* poster. 'Funny,' I say to Vincent. 'You never see any *Stronger in Europe* posters, do you? When I drove up to Harwich yesterday, it was Leave, Leave, Leave all the way.'

'I haven't been looking. Only got eyes for you, darling.'

He's such a poppet.

The EU Referendum is tomorrow. Another thing about which I haven't made up my mind. It's just too full of other things.

The rain has eased off by the time we arrive back home, bathing my garden in pale but determined sunshine. My borders don't look so good this year, as I've had no time, even for weeding, but fortunately the crimson rhododendrons and deep red peonies are thriving on my neglect. One of the reasons I retired was to have more time for growing vegetables and tending my roses, but it hasn't worked out that way.

Vincent steps across the soggy lawn with the shopping bags, on tiptoe so as not to dirty his 'see your face in' shiny, leather, lace-up shoes. I believe Mother polishes them for him.

Following him into the kitchen, I wrap my arms around his waist. 'I'm so happy.'

We kiss like love-struck teenagers doing it for the first time. 'I'm dying for a coffee,' he says at last, unravelling his arms and stepping over to the kettle. 'I went to the health food shop with Mother this morning. She wanted to buy some more of that special Peruvian coffee. They grind it fresh on the premises, you know. I got some for us as well.' He thrusts a tiny gold-foil packet under my nose. 'Smell that.'

'Mm, delicious,' I say, even though, hitherto, I've been a tea-drinker.

'Want some?'

'Yes, please. Did you call in at the gallery?'

'No.'

'Your paintings are in there. If you're going to make a sale…'

'I don't like to bother them. My art must speak for itself, darling.'

I unpack the shopping. 'I've got some of those heritage tomatoes.' I hold up the cellophane-wrapped pack to show him, realising suddenly how knobbly and unappetising they look.

He's doing his theatrical barista act, cascading milk into our mugs from a great height.

I laughed for five minutes the first time he did it a month ago, but this morning I wish he'd just glance at these heritage tomatoes and say something nice about them. I catch sight of the price label. 'Bloody hell, Vincent. £4.45 a kilo.'

'Here's your coffee, darling.' He sits down at the kitchen counter with his own cup. 'I'll get us some proper tomatoes on Saturday. Mother knows this wonderful market stall in Cavenham. All fresh.'

'I see.' I throw *my* tomatoes into the salad box at the bottom of fridge; they land with a thud, bruising them probably. 'Bloody waste of time and money then, wasn't it?'

Vincent stares at me, his hands outstretched. 'Tomatoes, Julie, just tomatoes.'

We have a row, our first. I wrench open the fridge door. I contemplate hurling the spurned red fruit in his face. Or, better still, smashing them against the tiled wall. I'd wrench my arm back as far as possible, then fling them, watching them squash on impact, watery brown juice and yellow seeds dripping down the paintwork. But I don't. Sensible Julie doesn't do that sort of thing.

As our words lose their energy, the feeble sun fades away. In its place comes premature evening gloom, and rain, such rain, beating upon the windows like granite pellets. It would last all night and into the following morning. We say our sorries. He says I get too intense about things and I suppose I do. I didn't used to.

'There're more important things,' he says, 'like voting in the EU Referendum tomorrow.'

'Yes, I know.'

'Mother's going to vote Remain. She doesn't like Boris or that Michael Gove.'

The following morning, the torrent forces us to drive to the polling station, even though it's only at the bottom of our road. As is required by law, the village hall doors are wide open, but the musty odour, overlain with toilet cleaner, nevertheless lingers in the rain-spattered hallway. Every polling station smells the same, but at least I'm no longer stuck all day behind some rickety folding table watching the square black ballot box, as I used to be when I was serving as a presiding officer. I did it for thirty odd years, making decisions, dealing with proxies, tendered votes and keeping tellers from the various political parties outside, even when it was chucking it down, as it is today.

We wait in the queue at the issuing desk. This is it. I have to decide. All the politicking will have to stop. In a minute, I must put my cross on one box or another.

'Mother's going to vote Remain,' Vincent says – again.

I met Mother for the first time when she invited me to Sunday lunch. We got talking about the forthcoming Referendum and I mentioned some of the arguments for and against leaving the European Union. I mentioned that this was what was being said in my office before I retired. 'Oh yes,' said Mother. 'Vincent tells me you had this little bean-counting job.'

I had been Director of Financial Control at the Borough Council, but that afternoon I was too much in love to respond.

When the poll clerk issues our ballot papers, I lean across the table to check that she has scored lines against our names on the Corresponding Numbers List. I can't help myself.

Now I'm standing in the polling booth, passing my ballot paper from one hand to the other. Voting is private, like using the lavatory. These tiny wooden booths resemble lavatories, although, I expect – never having built a toilet cubicle myself – that they're more tricky to erect. So many presiding officers' and poll clerks' fingers trapped over the years. But I'm letting my thoughts wander. I must vote. It's my duty as a British subject. I lower my hand. I touch the Remain box with my pencil – almost. I lift it.

In the neighbouring cubicle, I hear the rustle of paper, Vincent refolding his ballot slip. *Having voted as instructed by Mummy, no doubt.*

For ten minutes I hovered and wavered by the tomato

counter in Waitrose, trying to please him – or Mother. Digging my pencil into the paper and almost tearing it, I draw a heavy cross in the *Leave the European Union* box. My reasons are at least as good as his.

Vincent wakes me at seven o'clock the following morning, to tell me the Referendum result. Seventeen million voters haven't taken Mother's advice.

I'm shocked. I was not expecting it. I feel a teensy-weensy bit guilty, but not for long.

He makes me coffee in bed before setting off for Mother's, who is 'Very Upset'. He's spoken to her on the telephone several times already.

I listen to the sound of his car engine fading into the distance. He must, of course, rush off to the most important woman in his life. I get up and pour my coffee – his coffee – down the loo. I tear the covers off the bed and toss them downstairs. As I eat my breakfast, of grilled heritage tomatoes on toast, swilled down by tea, I watch the sheet, pillowcases and duvet-cover churning around in the washing machine.

I place the opened, gold-foil, packet of 'special' coffee 'ground fresh on the premises' on the window ledge by the front door. He can take it to Mother's when he calls for his things. I know why we're both single, and why we need to remain that way.

Ella's Holiday

Ella wished they'd stop talking. Dirty grey drifts lingered at the perimeter of the school playground, without even a budding snowdrop to challenge them, but already the talk in the school staffroom was about summer holidays. At the next desk Debbie was surfing the internet. Ella glimpsed whitewashed villas, purple bougainvillea, and an impossibly turquoise swimming pool. With an effort, she picked up her pen and continued marking.

'This is where we're going in Tenerife,' said Debbie, swivelling the screen around, just as Ella was settling back into 10B's essays on Dickens. 'The children are going to love it. Be in the pool all day.'

'Lovely,' said Ella, without looking up.

'Gets up to twenty-five degrees in July.' Debbie hugged her skinny chest with her folded arms, crushing the raw linen top everyone had admired that morning. 'Gosh, it's so cold in here.'

Ella, wearing two jumpers and other, unmentionable, layers underneath, felt just right.

'Turn the heater on, will you, Antonia?' Stretching over her colleague, Debbie flicked the heater switch herself.

Bracing herself for a blast of hot air, Ella edged her chair sideways.

'Sorry. What did you say?' Antonia clicked off her CD player and lifted her headphones from her ears. 'I'm trying to learn Russian. Did I tell you we're going to Russia in July?'

Yes, you did, several times, thought Ella. In fact, over the last few days, Antonia had given them a running commentary on the booking of her holiday and now she was doing it again. Ella anticipated every word. After Moscow, it was the Trans-Siberian Railway to Ekaterinburg... where the Tsars were murdered, you know... then on to the Hermitage in St Petersburg. In a minute, her colleague would list the works of art on view there. Ella considered buying noise-cancelling headphones, but then reflected that they probably wouldn't work.

'I couldn't be doing what you're doing,' said Debbie, picking up Antonia's CD. 'It says on here that you should be speaking 'travellers' Russian' in six weeks. Everyone in Tenerife knows English. That's one of the reasons why we keep going there.'

'Russian's a beautiful language,' said Antonia. 'And how else do you absorb the culture?'

'You can't do culture with teenagers,' said Debbie.

'Of course you can.'

'No, you can't.'

'We took our children to Florence when they were six and seven. They went round all the museums and churches with us. And they thoroughly enjoyed it. It depends what you want from a holiday, Debbie.'

Debbie opened her mouth to answer but Antonia had rendered herself incommunicado again by replacing her headphones. If Barbara had still been here, she and Ella would have exchanged raised eyebrows, with Barbara intoning 'miaow' in an undertone. Instead, Ella concentrated on correcting a pupil's spelling of 'receive': I before E except after C. No one expected Ella to hold a view. She carried on marking, with just the usual staffroom sounds burbling in the background; the gentle hum of voices, the clatter of cups upon the tea tray and the clunk-clunk of the fridge being opened and shut.

All too soon the bell rang for the beginning of afternoon school. The teachers made for the door with pupils' work piled high in the cardboard lids of printer paper boxes, which they used for filing trays. Picking up her pencil case, a class set of handouts and a tatty cardboard wallet on which she had written 'Hamlet Worksheet 1' in neat handwriting, Ella sneaked a glance at her holdall under her desk. Inside it a bright pink cover glowed through its flimsy plastic W H Smith carrier. She took two steps from her desk. She halted. She went back. She reached under her desk and zipped up her holdall, before rushing out the staffroom with the others. Miss Pritchard was never late for class.

'Actually you might like Tenerife, Ella,' said Debbie, as they clambered up the stairs amidst the hurly-burly of children texting on mobiles and playing on hand-held games consoles. 'There are parts of it which are very quiet.'

Ella smiled. That's what they thought of her.

As she was climbing into her car at the end of the school day, Ella's mobile rang. Weary, thinking of what she would eat tonight – something which wouldn't take too long to prepare – she almost pretended she hadn't heard.

'Ella, it's me. Did you call earlier? I've just been for an amazing walk across the fields in the snow.'

'Oh, hello, Barbara.'

'Now, did you manage to buy the ordinance survey map?'

'Oh yes.' It scorched a pink hole in her bag. As she struggled through the afternoon traffic, Ella asked herself why she had rushed out to buy a map in her free period when Barbara, who was retired, had been rambling across the country for pleasure.

Winter melted into spring – crocuses, daffodils, tulips. Over Easter, Debbie and Antonia visited France together with their families and returned with the inevitable photographs, Debbie in front of the Eiffel Tower, Antonia against a backdrop of rippling blue water. 'That's the Lake, Ella,' Antonia said. 'Lake Geneva.'

'As if I'd never seen such a thing before,' Ella said to Barbara, as they drove to book club that evening.

Her friend groaned. 'I know, dear.'

'Then she explained that she had taken the photo in a place called 'Thonon Les Bains'. She pronounced it very slowly. It's a town, Barbara, in France. Poor, pathetic Miss Pritchard couldn't be expected to know where France was, now could she?'

'Don't let them get to you.'

'Oh no. Known them too long. They're all right really. Do you want to see my new Kindle?'

Spring became summer – alyssum, cornflowers, sweet peas, then at last the roses, their heavy scents wafting in through the open windows of the staffroom. Exams invigilated and marking done, the pupils gone, just the paperwork remained. Ella entered her results on to a spreadsheet while Antonia tidied her desk, chucking out dog-eared pieces of work by pupils who were about to leave. The 'learn Russian' CD slipped out of a pile of old handouts about Henry VIII and on to the floor. As she stared down at the sleeve, Antonia's mouth curled and her shoulders heaved themselves into a tight shrug. 'Too late now. We're flying on Saturday.' She threw the CD away, the plastic case hitting the metal bin so hard that it wobbled.

Debbie burst into the staffroom, her phone clasped against her ear. 'No, darling, it's not going to be boring. We've got the pool, haven't we?' She switched on the kettle as she spoke. 'But you like swimming.' The furrows on her face deepened as she wrestled, one-handed, with the brown plastic cap on her Nescafe jar. 'No, you can't stay at home. Hang on...' She shoved her phone in front of her eyes, her glare bouncing against the tiny screen. 'The little madam's hung up on me.' She stomped over to her desk in four large, straight-legged strides. 'She doesn't want to go. My daughter is refusing to go on holiday with us.'

'Well, you know, Debbie, she's fifteen now,' said Antonia. 'Not a child anymore.'

'I do know how old my own daughter is, thank you very much, Antonia.'

Silence. Other teachers listened and watched, with lowered heads, pretending not to. After a moment Ella stood up, walked across the staffroom, finished making Debbie's coffee and handed it to her.

'Thanks,' she said, gripping her mug so hard that her knuckles became white. Tears spilled from her glistening eyes, rolling down her cheeks. 'Sorry,' she muttered. 'Sorry.'

'She'll enjoy it when she gets there,' Ella said, passing over the tissue box which they kept for pupils who turned on the waterworks. 'She's doing what teenagers do: testing the boundaries. She'd be scared if you did let her stay at home.'

Debbie gave the tiniest of nods.

'You'll have a wonderful holiday in Tenerife,' Ella said.

'Of course, you will,' said Antonia.

'And you'll have a great time in Russia, Antonia,' Ella added. 'Don't worry about not knowing the language. How could you possibly learn it when you're teaching full time, and doing all the wretched paperwork? You'll have a tour guide. He or she will show you around.'

Antonia rolled her eyes. 'Stout ladies from Intourist, ex-KGB, saying, "This is where the Socialist comrades shot the Imperialist Romanoffs. Look now, please." '

'It'll be very interesting,' said Ella.

'Where are you going, Ella?' asked Debbie, sniffing and wiping her face. 'Somewhere nice, I hope.'

'Oh yes.'

The morning after the end of term Ella had a lie-in, even though the sun started pouring through her curtains, making criss-cross patterns on her light summer duvet, from five o'clock onwards. The only thing that did take her downstairs was wanting a cup of tea, which she drank, standing up in her kitchen, watching the feathery ears of corn fluttering in the field opposite. She listened to the radio as she did her chores. 'Oh dear, oh dear,' she murmured on hearing that traffic on all motorways to Heathrow, Gatwick and Stansted was gridlocked. The phone rang while she was opening the fridge to survey what remained inside it. 'Hello there,' said Barbara. 'Free at last, eh?'

'Oh yes.'

'We need to talk about tomorrow; I'm going to pick you up at eight.'

'Yes, that's what we agreed last week.' Ella was cutting bread for her toast with her phone pressed against her ear.

'Have you got sun cream?'

'Oh yes.'

'We need factor 30 at least, if we're going to be out walking all day. Could you—'

'I've got factor twenty-five, which I think is sufficient for Northumberland. See you tomorrow, Barbara.'

'At eight, prompt.'

'Oh yes.' Ella put the phone down as she took her toast out the toaster, lightly browned, just as she liked it. How wonderful it was not to have to rush breakfast.

Half an hour or so later, Ella closed the front door of her little terraced house and made her way down the main street of her village, pausing at the church, as she always did, to enjoy the blues, pinks and yellows of the flowers in the churchyard. No gardener, she didn't know what they were, but she recognised their sweet fragrance, which, for years now, she had called the 'end of term smell'. She climbed up the hill, alongside a field of wispy barley, over a wooden stile and through set-aside land dotted with white and yellow daisies and dandelions.

Stopping at last by a big oak tree, she laid her checked travelling rug at the foot of its trunk and sat down, leaning against its soft corky trunk. She took out her Kindle and read a novel which was not on any school English syllabus. In the distance, she could just about make out the sound of cars, a soft drone above the rustling of the wind through the grass and the hum of insects.

Next week she and Barbara would walk Hadrian's Wall; like Debbie's daughter in Tenerife, she would enjoy it when she got there. But today she would watch the furry bees as they crept into purple bells of wild foxgloves, their rotating wings rippling through the air like tiny propellers, and a frumpy brown mother duck, with six downy chicks, waddling by the river.

Ella's holiday had begun.

Never Too Old, Never Too Young

My phone beep-beeps. I'm not even going to look. It'll be a selfie of Hannah in a bikini beside a deep blue swimming pool in Greece. Or Chloe eating ice cream under a sun-bleached parasol in a café in Cancun. Or Elouise telling me how hot she is in Florida. I don't want to know.

I'm stuck here at home. Nobody's around and there's nothing to do except look out my bedroom window. People say I'm lucky to live in a nice village like Wapheton, but I've been sitting here all summer, hoping something will happen, and nothing does here in Suffolk. It's not fair. We never go anywhere. Except Norfolk. Norfolk doesn't count.

The artificial fragrance of cheap fabric conditioner, the sort that glugs into the washing machine like gloopy blue yoghurt, fills my room as Mum enters, her arms full of folded towels. 'Sarah, Sarah,' she says, 'please put these in the guest room. Quick.'

'Have we got punters?' I lever myself off the window-ledge, as if I have all the time in the world. I have, actually.

Someone's banging on the door.

'Sarah, Sarah. Bed and breakfast visitors, please.' Mum shakes her head at me.

'Whatever.'

Dad bought the heavy brass knocker from an antique shop in the village, the Christmas before he left. Bang, bang, bang. The noise of that knocker on our door reverberates through the whole house, shaking the old beams and shattering the lath and plaster. Every day, Mum sweeps up bits of wall.

I drape the towels on the radiator in the guest-room, then dart back to my window-ledge. I've no intention of being around while Mum shows the punters upstairs, makes small talk about the weather, and finds out what they want for breakfast – hopefully, not the full English which we advertise. I can't understand why anyone wants to come and have a holiday in Wapheton, but they do, usually old people. They take photos of the thatched cottage opposite, pick their way over our cobbled streets, take cream teas in the *tea shoppes* and buy things in the *gifte shoppes*. They potter around our medieval 'wool church', ooh and aah at the blue and red stained glass windows, gawp at the vaulted ceiling, then hobble down the stone steps to the crypt where lie various saints whose names I've forgotten, even though we did a project on the church at primary school. I know what a 'wool church' is though. Not that complicated. It's a church built by prosperous wool merchants.

I heave a sigh. At last Mum's finished her spiel, so maybe I'll go downstairs and get a biscuit.

Gran is watching a nature programme in the lounge. 'Look at these birds. Aren't they beautiful? This is Peru, love.' Gran adores this sort of thing, anything foreign. I sit and watch with her for a while, until my stomach reminds me of my original reason for leaving my usual lair.

In the kitchen, Mum, small beads of perspiration forming on her red face, is rushing around preparing the evening meal. I offer her the open biscuit tin. 'I shouldn't,' Mum replies, taking two, 'but our B&B guest's ordered dinner. It's half past five and I've only just started cooking. And she wants the full English tomorrow morning. She's American, says she wants the full Brit experience, whatever that is.'

'It's all money, Mum.' Dad left us with this house and as little else as he could get away with. A clean break, the solicitor called it. It's certainly breaking my mum.

She crams the second custard cream into her mouth. 'I know. I know. She's staying four nights. I don't know how I'm going to cope with cooking evening meals for four nights, and cleaning at the pub, but we'll manage somehow. I keep telling myself that in a fortnight, we'll be in Norfolk.'

I say nothing.

'We'll be sitting in Auntie Janice's cottage, you, Gran and I, watching the world go by. You can go on the beach.'

My shoulders slump. 'And build sandcastles with my bucket and spade? Mum, I am not a baby.'

'Well, Sarah,' she says, leaning down to pull the bag out the kitchen bin, 'we can't afford anything else.' She stomps out the back door to the dustbin.

Oh, why do I always say the wrong thing? I check Mum's eyes, when she comes back, to make sure she's not crying. 'Auntie Janice's cottage has got quite good Wi-Fi. Shall I set the table?'

'Yes please.'

I open the cutlery drawer and start counting out knives, forks and spoons. 'Just one punt... person, Mum?'

'Yes. She's by herself.' They usually come in couples. A single person in a double room is not a good deal for us. My mum, she's too nice.

After doing the table, I mooch back into the lounge where Gran is now making conversation with the 'punter', a tall blonde woman perched on the edge of the other chair. 'Hi, I'm Chrissie. From Texas. You must be Sarah. I've heard all about you from your Gran.'

'Chrissie's an air stewardess. Flight attendant as they say in America,' says Gran. 'She flies all over the world. Don't you, dear?'

Chrissie nods, her smile extending from one dangly earring to the other.

I hate Chrissie.

Gran leans forward in her chair, drinking up our punter's talk of all the many places she's visited. I don't want to listen. I really don't want to listen to more travel stories. But I can't be bothered to move either. I sit staring at the tiny sparkly mirrors on her denims, wondering whether I could buy some and sew them on to my own jeans. When Chrissy stops talking, eventually, to draw breath, I say, 'I want to be a flight thingy.'

'Sure. Apply to one of the British airlines. When you're older. I guess you have to be eighteen. How old are you now, Sarah?'

'Fifteen.'

'Only three years, then.'

Three long years of this place. Wapheton sticks to me like glue. 'Where do you actually live, Chrissie? New York? LA?' San Fran? Do Americans say 'San Fran'? I'm trying to sound cool, but I suspect I'm off the mark.

'Sharon Plains, Texas, is my hometown. Hicksville. You won't know it.'

'Where's Hicksville?'

The black liner around the rims of Chrissie's brown eyes roll for a millisecond. 'Two gas stations, two motels, three diners, two Baptist churches, one Presbyterian and a whole lot of trailers. That's Sharon Plains.'

'Hicksville isn't a real place, love,' Gran tells me, after Chrissie's gone upstairs. 'It's what we in England call "the back of beyond".'

'Like this village then?'

Gran, originally from the East End of London, lays her hand on my shoulder. 'You'll get to go abroad, love. One day. You're young. You can work for it. Can't you?'

I know that tone and that turn of phrase. 'Yes, Gran. I know.'

'You have to work for everything in this life. Like your poor mum does. Now, give me my crutches, please, love. I need the loo.'

I help her haul herself out of her chair and balance her tiny brittle frame on her crutches. 'But everyone else in my class—'

'Never mind everyone else in your class. As I said... one day. Go and help your mum, darlin.' She's rushing around as usual.'

I don't hate Chrissie. I like her a lot, actually. She's been to all these fantastic places, but she's doing it for work, so I don't mind when she talks about it. Her clothes are amazing. On Sunday she comes downstairs wearing this turquoise shift dress with matching high-heeled shoes. 'My mom says you should look your best for God,' she says, as we set off for church, and there's me in my usual t-shirt and jeans, although in a minute I'll have my black choir gown on.

After the service Chrissie insists on viewing every bit of our famous and massive 'wool church', and taking photos, long after Mum has driven Gran home in the car. 'So purdy,' she says. 'Everything in Suffolk's so purdy. Is Norfolk purdy too?'

I shrug.

'You're going there for your vacation.'

'We go every year.' Just thinking of it made me well up with tears.

'Oh honey,' says Chrissie squeezing my arm and handing me a tissue. 'I know, I know. My family don't want to go any place either. They say they have everything they need in Sharon Plains. Whoa.' She grabs the railing. 'My heels don't do British cobbles.'

'I so want to travel like you do. Gran says I have to work for it, but I can't take even a part-time job until next year when I'm sixteen.'

'I flipped burgers at my cousin's diner all through high

86

school. Wouldn't Mom pay you to do chores for your paying guests?'

I shook my head several times. 'She's got no money… Chrissie!' She grabs at my arm as she goes down. 'Are you all right?'

There is a long silent moment before she says, 'Sure,' so quietly I can hardly hear her. She's not all right at all, lying face down on the pavement with blood seeping from a white gash over her eye.

'Oh… er.' *Come on, Sarah. You did first aid at school last year.* I try to pull Chrissie to her feet, but she's leaning against me and crying out when I tell her to put her foot down. And she's really heavy, because she's tall, I suppose. She slips from my hold, her knees folding like a deck chair as she slides down against the yellow sandstone wall of the church, back on the pavement, her lovely turquoise dress marked with chalky yellow dust.

'Tired.' Her eyes are closing. 'Real tired.'

'No, Chrissie, no. Don't go to sleep. Please.' *Gash on head… concussion. Concussion patients must stay awake.* That's what they taught us in first aid. 'Chrissie, Chrissie, open your eyes.'

'I'm… fine.'

'No, you're not. Chrissie, stay awake. Er… I'm ringing Mum.' I'm really scared, but Mum says keeping Chrissie awake is the right thing to do and she'll call an ambulance. Twenty minutes it is before it arrives, and I am, like, responsible. Afterwards, we walk home carrying the turquoise high heeled shoe which had got itself stuck in the cobbles.

When Mum fetches Chrissie from hospital, late that evening, her face is grey and her ankle strapped up. She's strained a ligament and needs to rest it. 'I'm real sorry. Do you want me to stay someplace else?'

'No, no,' says Mum. 'Just get yourself right. Fancy a cup of tea?'

'Y'all are real kind.'

'I'm very sorry for her,' says Mum next day, 'but she's in a double room and I'm charging her single rate. What happens if Pam from Tourist Information rings up wanting us to take a couple? Or even a family?'

'We'd have to say no,' says Gran.

'We need the money,' says Mum.

I bolt back to my room and my window. I know what she means. I know what I ought to do. It's raining today, so there are only a few people around, a mother, father and two children entering Tourist Information, but I open my casement anyway and look out for what may be the last time for a while.

Downstairs the phone's ringing. 'Hello Pam,' says Mum.

With a long sigh which blows the ivy leaves on the wall outside, I shut my window and rummage around the junk on my bedside table. Scribbling something on an old envelope, I rush downstairs and push my message in front of my mother's eyes.

'Are you sure?' Mum mouths as she reads.

I nod.

'Thank you, Sarah,' says Mum, as we dust and hoover my room. 'Thank you so much.'

'I don't mind Chrissie being in here.'

Mum and I sleep on the sofa bed that night. We get up at six o'clock in the morning, clear away our bedding and prepare breakfast for five guests: Chrissie, and the four members of family who I saw walking into Tourist Information yesterday. They're in Mum's room and mine. Actually, I quite enjoy bustling around in an apron, serving breakfast, and being with Mum.

At last we're done and sitting in the kitchen, drinking tea. 'Chrissie said I might do jobs for you and get paid for them, but I'd never ask you for money, Mum.'

'Sorry, love. Got nothing to give you.'

For several days Chrissie watches television with Gran, her ankle raised on a stool, an unfortunate end to her holiday. She was intending to visit Stratford-upon-Avon and Scotland before flying back to Dallas at the end of the week. On her last night she orders us Chinese takeaway as a thank you for looking after her.

'Y'all come visit me in Texas,' she says, like she is inviting us across the road for afternoon tea.

I dig my spoon into one of the plastic containers. 'Ooh yes please, Chrissie.'

Mum shoots me a warning glance.

'It's all right, Mum. I'll save up. All my birthday money and next summer when I'm sixteen I'll get a job.'

'Uh-huh.' Chrissie shakes her head. 'I was thinking of right now, within the next few weeks. I figure Sarah has school in September.'

Mum puts down her fork, the red sauce oozing off the chunk of sweet and sour pork she's just speared. 'Chrissie, you must understand—'

'I sure do understand. I've been flat broke most of my life. But we flight attendants are allocated ten concessionary flights per year for friends and family. And my family are homebirds. They don't want to go no place. You guys fly *Air Texas* free on me.'

For a moment, there's silence. It is as if I'm not sitting at the table at all, but looking down from the ceiling at another Sarah. When I speak, at last, my voice sounds tinny, as if it belongs to someone else. I ask Chrissie to repeat, twice, three times.

'To America... Texas... in... before the beginning of

term.' Not here in this house. No window. No thatched cottages. No cobbles. Scary. Yes, well scary. For a moment, only a moment though, I don't want it. 'Oh, thank you, Chrissie. Thank you so much. Mum, we can go, can't we?'

'Oh, Chrissie, that's a wonderful offer,' says Mum after a long pause in which I dreaded saying her saying, 'couldn't possibly accept.' 'Thank you so much. Sarah is desperate to travel.'

'You and Mum'll have the best holiday ever,' says Gran, squeezing my knee.

'You too, ma'am.'

'But my legs...'

'No problem. All airlines nowadays can give assistance for people with... er... legs.'

'Are you sure? Gran's eyes fill with tears. 'I've wanted to go abroad all my life. Like Sarah. But I thought I was too old now.'

'Never too old, ma'am. And never too young.'

My Blue Period

Carl is calling Ben a prat and a wally and other insults on the tips of nine-year olds' tongues. I'm on the carpet, feeling under the coffee-table and the chairs.

Until a moment ago, we were watching *Match of the Day*, my two boys and me. I know it's late for them, but none of us can sleep these days. Our team, City, has just scored. We were leaping up from our seats, swinging our arms above our heads and screaming, 'Yes,' but, when Carl dropped back into his place on the settee, he sat on the remote and switched us over to *The News*.

I find the device wedged down the side of the cushions. I'm pressing buttons one by one. Is it the green one? The red one? Rick would've known, but Rick isn't here. Yes, it is the green one. We have football on the screen again, blue shirts jumping on top of one another. *Yes, yes, and really yes.* Blue scarves are being held aloft in the stands, their wearers chanting as one. We march around our living room singing with them, 'We're City. We're good. We're City. We're good.'

As ten o'clock waxes into half past, Carl dozes against my shoulder. I comb his silky childish hair through my fingers. I'm happy. I'm not used to being happy. Every night for the last six months, I've lain awake – and alone – in what used to be our double-bed, watching the hands creep around the clock and willing on the dawn, cold despite the winter duvet, my spine rigid against the mattress Rick and I chose together last summer. Yet tonight I fall asleep at once, with blue-shirted figures leaping about under my closed eyelids.

'You should get out more, Sally,' my mother says to me, after the boys and I have discussed football in her house for half an hour.

91

She suggests I find a job. To stop her nagging, I make some applications, although I've lost my confidence, having not been in paid employment since Ben was born. I accept a position as a receptionist in Outpatients at the General Hospital, but only because they're offering me shifts which finish in time for school pickup. Towards the end of my first morning, having signed form after form in human resources, and watched videos on Safeguarding, Prevent and British Values, I meet Lorraine, my line manager. 'Welcome to Hell.' She speaks in a monotone and without looking up from her computer.

'Galatasaray,' I say at once.

Lorraine's chair squeaks as she swings around to face me. 'Er... Galatasaray. Turkish football team. "Welcome to Hell" is their tagline.' I go bright red, like a schoolgirl. 'Er... Inappropriate. Sorry.'

'You like football?'

'It's just that I've got two boys and—'

'Football is life. The rest is mere detail.' Lorraine's voice becomes higher and louder, as Carl's does when something excites him. 'I've got that on a T-shirt, in Italian. I'll bring it and show it you tomorrow.' Sitting at her workstation behind the reception desk, with blue-shirted City players looking down on us from press cuttings, Lorraine and I chat about City throughout our lunch break. 'Clinic doesn't open until two,' Lorraine says to any patients who arrive early.

Later on, I take what seems like an eternity to check in my first patient on the computer, even with several colleagues looking over my shoulder, but I soon get the hang of it. I'm fine. We receptionists have lots of laughs, and Lorraine too. She's not like a boss at all. We talk football all the time.

I'm divorced now and Ben's started at secondary. On the first day, I shed a tear as I waved him off on the school bus.

How I wished I hadn't bought uniform in the next size up, because he looked so young with his blazer covering his bottom and his trousers over his heels. Now, at half-term, I'm glad I did, because he's growing so fast, and his voice is breaking. He's made some new friends, which is good, I suppose, although he and they rush straight upstairs to play computer games, so I don't get to meet them. I used to call up to them, offering Cola and biscuits, but Ben's asked me not to do it. 'Embarrassing, Mum.'

'My daughter used to say that,' Lorraine says, as she and I settle down on our settee to watch England's friendly against Germany on the television. She's brought a bottle of Prosecco but our national team gives us no cause for rejoicing that evening. Ben comes downstairs the minute Lorraine's out the door. 'Mu-um.'

'Er...' I'm hoarse from belting out 'Eng-er-la-and' for ninety minutes.

'Do you have to shout like that? You should just hear yourself.'

'Why didn't you come down and watch it with us, Ben, love?'

'I had my mates round, didn't I?

Lorraine's husband, Colin, is a hospital porter. He nods at her empty chair, as he clatters through Outpatients with an unoccupied trolley. 'Where's herself?

I shrug. 'Not far away'. She has a great many cigarette breaks, tea and coffee breaks these days.

'How're you? And your boys?'

'Okay.'

'Only okay? How old are they now?'

'Eleven and thirteen.'

'Oh-oh.' He leans on the trolley. 'Difficult ages, but they grow out of it. Our daughter was a stroppy little

93

madam from eleven onwards, but she's fine now. Good job. Even a boyfriend we like.'

I hang on to that conversation all day. I don't worry about Carl; he's joined the local drama group, and nowadays he comes home from school and does his homework straightaway, so he can get off to his rehearsals. Ben, I hardly see, even though he's always at home, in his room, his bed unmade and the curtains drawn, and on his computer. The day I spoke to Colin, I return from work to a house which might be deserted, despite my older son's schoolbag being dropped in the middle of the hall floor, ready for me to trip over. I didn't. I was used to it being there. I shout 'Hello,' several times but I hear no reply. Later on, I have to call him three... four... five times for his evening meal and, when he does deign to join Carl and me at the table, he pushes his plate away after a few mouthfuls and bolts back upstairs. I can deal with difficult patients at work, even those who are determined to make a complaint before they walk through the door, but I can't cope with my own Ben.

After washing-up, I switch on the telly. At least there's football. City versus Liverpool tonight. We score after five minutes. Liverpool hit the bar. Three times. *Torture*, texts Lorraine. Now, I'm willing time forward, desperate for the referee's final whistle. I was like that on the last occasion I went to see our team play at City Park. £50, my seat cost me, and I sat in it wishing away the ninety minutes by the second.

The following morning, I awake to Ben's fingers tap-tapping on his keyboard in his room. 'Good to see you up early, Ben, love.'

He grunts, his eyes fixed on the screen.

Then I catch sight of his ironing, in a neat pile on his duvet, in the exact place I left it the previous evening.

He says it's his life and none of my business if he doesn't go to bed. He's fed up with my nagging. He's going to live with his dad and his dad's girlfriend, who 'treat me like an adult.'

I ring Mum, in tears.

'At least you know where he is,' she says.

'I've tried, Mum. I've tried so hard. I watched football with them, taken them to matches.'

'Sally, he's grown out of football. It's you who hasn't.'

Ben's been gone a day... a week... two weeks... three weeks... I've failed him.

I'm struggling to keep cheerful for Carl, and at work. The General Hospital has new managers. All reception staff now report to this dreadful woman, Diane, who wears high heels and a pinstriped power suit with padded shoulders and who, I swear, has never set eyes on a real patient in her life. She keeps leaning over our Outpatients counter and staring at Lorraine's vacant chair. Diane's sent me for training on the new computer system, which I'm supposed to 'cascade down' to the other receptionists.

Lorraine snorts. 'Nothing wrong with the old system.' Her daughter's getting married in August and she's spending all her time looking up wedding dresses on the internet. 'Clinic doesn't start until two,' she calls over her shoulder to the 'customers' (as Diane insists we call them) congregating in the waiting room.

I look at the clock on the wall: one fifty.

We'd just checked in the first lot of 'patients' (as I still call them) when Diane summonses Lorraine to her office. My friend returns later with a face like a grey thundering sky and eyes flashing white darts of lightning. 'She's... given me... a verbal warning.' The words splutter from her.

I lead her away from the counter. I'm trying to be sympathetic but I'm not surprised.

She cries out in a football-stand bellow. 'I hate this place.'

'Ssh. The patients'll hear you.'

'I don't care.'

I take my purse from my handbag. 'We're going for an early tea break. Come on.'

As if she doesn't know her way, I steer her along the corridors to the canteen, and order two teas. When I set the steaming cardboard containers on our table, she's on her phone to Colin.

She cancels her call with a vicious prod. 'I really don't need this. I'm trying to organise a wedding. You're invited by the way.'

'Oh. Thank you.'

'Twentieth September. City're playing Man U that day. We can't miss Man U, can we? We'll just be a bit late for the reception.'

'Er… what?'

'The wedding's at one and will be over by two. It's only fifteen minutes to the stadium from the church.' She giggles. 'Football is life.'

'No.' I shake my head so hard it hurts. 'No. You've got a lovely husband and daughter. You are very lucky. Football is not life, Lorraine.'

My chair scrapes on the linoleum floor as I push it back, leaving her and my tea. 'Sally… Sally…' she calls after me as I march out, but I don't look back.

When I return to my desk in Outpatients, my mobile phone screen informs me I've missed three calls. From Lorraine, I suppose. Then I look again. 'Three missed calls from School' reads the message. All fingers and thumbs, I jab in my keycode, struggling to recall it through the red haze in my brain.

'Nothing to worry about,' says the school administrator, words calculated to strike terror in every parent's heart. 'Ben's had a bit of a knock in football this afternoon. The ambulance's just left.'

Ambulance?

School's just around the corner, and A&E at the opposite end of the hospital building. Making garbled apologies to my colleagues, I charge along corridors. Patients in pyjamas, outpatients with limbs in plaster, lost visitors peering at signs, doctors and nurses in uniform, all of them fade into a blur as I push through them. At A&E at last, I scan the figures sitting on hard chairs and watching daytime television: an elderly couple, a workman in overalls, a mother with a baby. *Not Ben, not Ben.*

I hear a whimper. 'Mu-u-um.'

I swing my head right. I swing my head left.

'Mum, I'm here.'

He's lying on a trolley, under a red ambulance blanket, his football socks poking out the bottom, smeared with mud. He's alive. He can talk.

The track-suited teacher standing beside him shuffles his feet. 'It's his arm. Took his full weight when he fell. He's in a bit of discomfort.'

'My arm huuurts.' Ben lifts the blanket to show me his swollen wrist. 'I hate football.'

I don't reply. Do I love the Beautiful Game still? I'm trying to work out what I do feel.

After the teacher left, Ben reaches over with his good arm and grasps my hand so tightly I'm hurting too. 'I'm so sorry, Mum,' he says above the insistent television giving me news I can't be bothered with. 'I'm so sorry. About everything. I want to come back home.'

'Please do, Ben. Please, please do.'

'I'm a prat and a wally. Mum, I'm going to change. Really, I am.'

So am I. My Blue Period is over.

Last Hot Chocolate in Mostar

Xavier swears they're looking for us. I tell him we're at a border and checking passports is what they do at borders.

His eyes fixed upon the line of cars ahead, he gulps water from a plastic bottle, forcing it down his gullet in three noisy swallows. Fifty vehicles, even more, stretch in front of us, along the straight road which leads out of Croatia and into Bosnia, stationary, except for when we all creep forward a few measly metres every minute or so. There are cars behind us too. Turning back wouldn't be an option.

'Two border controls,' he says, through a gurgling burp. He puts his hand in front of his mouth. 'I don't like this.'

In the distance I see the Croatian police in their navy blue uniforms, and beyond them the Bosnians in bright blue and yellow. They're just standing around. 'We'll be all right.'

'I don't like this,' he says a second time.

'It'll be worth it. Bosnia. Outside the EU. We won't have to run anymore. We can start to think about our future.' I put my hand on his thigh. 'I love you,' I say for the umpteenth time that day.

'I love you too. Whatever happens, I'll always love you.'

We continue to wait. Nothing happens. I watch other drivers walking along the roadside verge to a makeshift café, and back again carrying drinks steaming from polystyrene cups just like the ones from the vending machine at school. Xavier and I fell in love whilst drinking hot chocolate from flimsy containers like these. I reach for the door handle. 'Let's buy some hot chocolate.'

'No, Hannah, please.' He bangs the steering wheel with his open palm. 'It's not safe.'

He doesn't speak again until both sets of police have stamped our passports – without even looking at us, by the way. As we head along an empty road through green rolling mountains, we see a sign telling us that it's just thirty eight miles to Mostar. He swings me a sidelong glance. 'You know about the Bridge at Mostar?'

'The one the Croatians blew up in the Yugoslav War?

'Well done. Not many kids your age would know that.'

'I'm not like...' I do the quote thing with my fingers. 'Kids my age... am I? I'm mature. You said so.'

'I suppose you read up about the Bridge on Wikipedia. Like you do everything else.'

'Wikipedia's all right.'

'Hannah, we've been through this before. Not a valid and reliable source.'

'Oh shut up. You're just saying that because you're a history teacher.'

He looks away from me. I hate it when he does that.

'Do you still love me when I'm annoying?' I ask as we enter the city of Mostar.

We see burnt out shells of buildings, pitted with bullet holes, as if the war happened yesterday. Much more interesting than the Hitler stuff we have to do for GCSE, even Xavier's lessons. I used to hang around at the end of his classes, asking him questions, about history – honest. When I wanted feedback for my coursework, we went after school to Starbucks in town. Now we're here, in Mostar.

We're in dire need of currency, because, this morning, the Croatians refused to change Euros into Bosnian. An old man in dusty overalls, his tanned face as creased as the Xavier's linen jacket, beckons us into a parking space outside the Bank of Sarajevo. He spits at our backs when we don't tip. There're no British newspapers on the newsstand by the door of the bank. This is good. Yesterday,

I spotted my school photo on the front page of *The Daily Mail*, but that was many miles away in Dubrovnik. Now the woman bank clerk with bottle blonde hair and dark roots is lingering over Xavier's passport though, lifting it to the light, putting it down, then picking it up again. She turns around to speak to someone. I draw in my breath and hold it, so does Xavier. Then we see that a colleague is passing her coffee in a minute cup and water in a murky glass. She stops to drink it. At last, she hands Xavier a wad of Bosnian Marks.

It's spitting with rain by the time we reach the famous Bridge. I run my hand over its smooth stones, little droplets running over my fingers. I marvel at its pronounced hump. 'So-o medieval.'

'Rebuilt in... 2004,' he says with a grin, reading from the adjacent plaque.

I laugh and he laughs with me. When I wrap my arms around his neck, his flattened palms spread across my back as if to touch as much of me as possible, yet he kisses with his lips only. Once I tried with tongues, but he clamped his mouth tight shut. Suddenly, he pulls away. 'Water's getting on my jacket.'

He's anal about that thing, tells me it's his only one. At school he wears it with a tie, which hangs down in front of him like a plumb line. Makes him look well old. He insists on going into this museum, where we watch a loop-tape showing the Croatians shelling the old Bridge. Now I hate the nice lady with whom we stayed last night in Dubrovnik. When we venture outside again, the rain is pelting down in long grey fingers, gushing over the uneven cobbled stones. Before he has time to protest, I drag him across the road to a cafe.

'I don't like this,' he says, darting his eyes to the right and to the left, as we sit down. He says this all the time.

'For Goodness sake, Xavier. Relax, can't you?'

'Tourist joint.' He leans forward as if this term might offend someone.

'We're in Bosnia. You said we'd be okay in Bosnia.' I glare at him. 'I'm going to order some hot chocolate, seeing as you wouldn't let me have anything at the border.' A middle-aged woman, with a tour guide's badge pinned to her flowery top, is lifting a mug of frothy brown cocoa nectar to her mouth, but she holds it there, as she rabbits on and on about the Bridge. The heavy aroma hangs in the air. I could almost snatch it from her hand. I hope Xavier doesn't clock that she's speaking English, because right now the sound of our own language terrifies him.

A waitress appears with a pad, all smiles.

'Hot... chocolate... please?' I hold up two fingers. '*Dobry?*' This word, meaning 'good', covers most situations in Eastern Europe.

She nods. '*Dobry.*'

When I ask where the facilities are, she points down a narrow gloomy staircase. I pass Flowery Top as I squeeze my way between chairs, tables and people. It's a Laura Ashley blouse she's wearing; my mother has one like it.

The stench that assaults me on entering the lavatory cubicle is so gross I close my mouth. When I emerge, Flowery Top is standing opposite me. I hold the loo door open for her but she doesn't move.

'Hannah?' She speaks in that low tone adults use when they're telling you something you don't want to hear. 'Hannah Watkins?'

I reach over to the basin, where one dark hair clings to the once-white surface and a sodden tissue rests by the cold tap. 'No,' I say in a voice like a robot's.

She raises her eyebrows.

I continue rinsing my hands. *Keep calm, Hannah.*

'Your photo's all over the papers, the television and the internet.'

I look her straight in the eyes. 'You've got the wrong person.' *Keep calm, Hannah. Don't run, Hannah.*

'I don't think I have.' She sounds like a teacher. She must've been one once.

'No.' I try to make my voice sound normal.

Then I run, two, three steps at a time. At the top there's daylight and fresh air sweetened by rain. I hear the clink of knives and forks, the hissing of the coffee machine and the murmur of contented voices. Seeing my love, his skinny, angular back framed by his white plastic chair, I lunge across the café floor.

He's reading, immersed in the museum brochure, and on the table in front of him are our two steaming mugs of hot chocolate. For once, he's at peace.

'Xavier.' Words tumble about in my brain, too many syllables and too urgent to enunciate.

'What?' He shoves the leaflet into his pocket, as if it's illegal or something. 'What's happened? Then he looks over my shoulder. 'Oh shit. Shit, shit, shit.'

'Just keep smiling.' I know, without looking, that Flowery Top is making her way towards us. 'I'm not me and you're not you. Right?'

He leaps to his feet. 'I'm in such shit.'

I push him down into his seat. 'We can't run this time. Too late. She's too close.'

He springs up again. 'Who'll get banged up? You? Or me?

'Shut up. She'll hear us.' She's the other side of the next table. 'Man up, will you? We can't run this time.' We ran from Ravenna. And from Lake Bled.

She's here now.

I make myself smile. 'Leave us alone, will you?

'Come on, Hannah.'

I hold out my upturned palms. I meet her eyes. 'Leave. Us. Alone.' I'm about to turn towards Xavier, meaning to roll my eyes at him, when I hear chair legs grating on the floor, a heavy thud and plates smashing.

I spin round. 'No. No. Don't.' I try to clamber over his chair, but it topples over, its sharp-edged plastic legs jabbing into mine. I would've fallen on top of it but for Flowery Top steadying my arm.

Xavier's crumpled linen jacket trails out behind him as he hurtles down the street. He's running. Again. Shoving his way between holiday-makers and leaping over street-side stalls, he disappears behind a green and yellow striped awning. *Stop, stop, Xavier. Wait for me.*

I spot him again on the Bridge, his head thrust forward like a rider-less racehorse, but there are so many other people, and I now I've lost him. A bloke carrying a huge umbrella and taking photos is taking up all the space. I think of running after him, but he's too far away. I think I catch another glimpse of his tousled brown hair on the camel hump of the brick Bridge. But I don't know. Maybe it's someone else.

Bastard. Beside me, Flowery Top's pulling out a chair for me, the one that Xavier was sitting on. *You runaway bastard.* I bang my bottom on to the flimsy plastic seat so hard it judders backwards. 'What are you going to do to me?' I snap at my floral jailor. *You ran away and left me here with her.*

She just looks at me.

'It wasn't how you think, you know. We loved each other.' *You said you loved me. You said that, whatever happened, you'd always love me.* All my clothes and other stuff are in his car.

She casts her eyes around the café, at her tour group members, then at the phone in her hand.

I feel the blunt round edges of my passport in my jeans pocket. 'I think I'll go home now. Back to the UK.' *You were running away so fast you never even looked back to see if I was behind you.*

'Ye-es,' she says. 'Yes, you must.'

'You don't need to worry about me anymore. I'm going to ring my mother and she'll arrange everything.' I speak very fast as I grope around in my bag for my phone. Then I notice the hot chocolate, which Xavier and I ordered a few minutes ago. I catch a whiff of its wicked fragrance, even though the shimmering white bubbles burst long ago. I reach across the table. I sluice the tepid brown fluid down my throat, first one mug, then the other, but how come it's so bitter in my mouth, so slimy on my tongue? Why ever did I think I liked this stuff?

Looking for Our House

'There it is,' said Nicky, jabbing her finger at the windscreen. 'Ooh look, Richard, look. Just like the photo in the brochure.'

Grabbing the estate agent's particulars, Nicky leapt out the car and strode across the road. Three terraced cottages nestled together like old friends, gnarled stems of ancient ivy clinging to their walls, with the evening sun lighting up their slate roof tiles. In the garden of the middle property stood a 'for sale' board.

The latch on the wrought-iron gate opened with a satisfying click. Bees hummed around lavender bushes along the path leading to the front door. 'Ah,' said Nicky, drawing the heavy scent into her nostrils. Then again, 'Ah.' She grabbed Richard's arm. 'Come on. I have a good feeling about this one. This is going to be *our house*.'

'Hang on. We haven't seen inside yet.' He rang the doorbell. 'Funny name, "Croit Chatreeney".'

'I read in the brochure this afternoon, that it's Manx and means "Kate's Cottage".'

'Manx? This isn't the Isle of Man.'

Nicky could have fallen in love with the cottage all over again while they were viewing the interior. 'It's beautiful,' she told Josh, the estate agent, who had shown them round. She wanted to add, 'We're going straight back to the office. Now. To make an offer.'

'Er… yes… thank you,' said Richard.

'Well?' asked Nicky the instant they were through the gate.

He didn't reply.

They climbed into the car. 'Well?'

'It was lovely.' He put his key into the steering column. 'Not was. Is.'

'More than we can afford, love.' He smiled that slow

smile of his, dimples on either side, which filled his square jaw, but did not extend beyond it.

'Only just above our price range. We could make an offer.' The energy in her words seemed to bounce off that smile.

'Not one they'd accept.'

'But…'

'No, Nicky, no.' As he eased into the road, he tilted his chin upwards and slightly to the right, a gesture she knew all too well.

When Josh rang Nicky at work next morning to ask how they liked the house, she said they were still thinking. He warned her not to wait too long, as he had other clients scheduled to view that evening. 'Don't let them,' she wanted to cry down the phone.

Aargh, Richard. She would talk to him again. As soon as possible. She knew she was right about this. The trouble with Richard was he dug his heels in, always had done. Even at primary school, there had been things Richard wouldn't do, country dancing, for instance. She would never forget that incident.

'Come along, Richard,' Miss Wilson had said. 'You can be Nicky's partner.'

Nicky'd tapped her barred shoe on the tiled floor of the school hall. She and the other children were already lined up, ready to start the 'Gay Gordons', and had been waiting for several minutes. 'Richard's a big wally,' she'd said to the girl standing next to her.

He, however, had remained rooted to the spot, tilting his chin to the right. At ten years old, he had been a miniature version of his adult self, thick-set with a square jaw and rectangular face.

'Do come along, Richard,' their teacher had gone on. 'We

106

haven't got all day. Don't you want to be in the dancing display at the fete?'

By now the class had fallen silent, making not a murmur, not a movement, for fear of missing something.

'Not really.'

The instant she replaced the receiver after speaking to Josh, the phone rang again. 'Can we meet up for lunch?' Richard's voice was just about audible. 'It's important.'

She knew that already. Richard didn't waste his almost silent tone on trivial matters.

She joined him at the pub down the road from the factory where he worked. She was just opening her mouth to tell him about her conversation with Josh, and how they needed to make an offer on *Croit Chatreeney* right away, when he said, 'Nicky, Woolton's are making people redundant.'

'Oh.' She laid her hands over his clenched knuckles. 'You?'

'I won't know for definite until next month, but...' He looked at her from under his hooded eyes. 'I heard this morning about a company advertising for skilled electricians. In Saudi Arabia.' His words hung in the air.

'Saudi?' The bar, the barman and the rainbow colours of the drink bottles danced a gig in front of her eyes. Richard had come back into her life about a year ago, when he had walked into the doctors' surgery where she worked as a receptionist. Watching him at the counter, filling in forms to register as a patient, she'd known his face but hadn't been able to place him. He'd recognised her straightaway. When he'd told her he'd been in the army, she'd pictured soldiers on parade being called to 'atten-shun' and one asking, in a mild voice, 'Why?' No longer children, they had hit it off immediately.

'Two year contract, Nicky,' he said. 'That's all.'

107

She forced herself to smile. 'Is it what you want to do?'

'Looks like I don't have much choice.' He shrugged. 'I'd be all right. I can do heat. And desert. I've been to Afghan, haven't I?

She struggled to keep smiling. 'When would you have to go?'

'Not sure. Quite soon.'

He stared at a beer mat in front of him, tracing its tight scalloped edge with his thick, stubby finger. In the background, the jukebox played *Waterloo* by Abba, a song Nicky used to like. 'Would you... would you... come to Saudi?'

'Of course I will.' Her words spluttered from her like an explosion, the sweetness of her orange juice catching the back of her throat.

'We wouldn't be able to have the sort of wedding we've been thinking of. We'd have to get married quickly. Within the next couple of months.' He leant forward. 'We'd be living on a compound, with the other Western workers. From what I've heard, we'd have a one-bedroomed flat. Nothing like *Croit Chatreeney*, I'm afraid.'

'We'd be together. That's the important thing.'

The two years in the Middle East passed quickly. When they returned, Woolton's were doing much better and Richard was offered a job as a foreman. With baby Jessica, they went to stay temporarily with Nicky's mother, but conditions were cramped, especially as one family member was taking up all the space in their room with her huge boxes of nappies, changing mat, Moses basket, car-seat and other paraphernalia. The heavy rain, which started on the Saturday morning of their first weekend in England, was a novelty – to start with.

Richard spent a large part of Sunday afternoon watching from the window, with Jessica asleep on his shoulder. He was not a man for sitting around. 'We do need a place of our own,' he kept saying.

'Let's start looking now,' Nicky replied, picking up her laptop and typing into Google the name of the first estate agent she remembered. For several moments she watched the hour-glass until, at last, a list of properties with photos appeared on screen, just one dull, boxy house after another. Then, suddenly, there appeared a slate-tiled roof glowing in the sunlight and a wrought-iron gate, with yellow hollyhocks framing the front door.

'Oh,' Nicky gasped. 'Oh.'

'What?' He peered at the screen from over the baby's head.

'The hollyhocks weren't there when we went before,' said Nicky.

'N-no,' he said at last.

She frowned. *No what? No hollyhocks? Or no, he wasn't interested.* She clambered to her feet. 'Fancy a cup of tea?' She had to think this through.

She took her time in the kitchen, taking a mug to Mum and stopping to chat with her. When she re-joined Richard, he was still looking at the tiny photo of *Croit Chatreeney* on the screen. 'You really loved that place, didn't you?' He lifted his head to meet her eyes.

'But you didn't.'

'I never said that.' Furrows formed on his brow. 'It was too expensive for us back then. We've got more money now, after Saudi. Do you want to see it again?'

'Of course.'

When Nicky rang the estate agent, it was Josh who answered the phone. He told her that the person who had bought *Croit Chatreeney* two years ago had been forced to move after only a year because of his job. *How disappointing to have to give up something so beautiful,* thought Nicky. All day long, as she fed and changed her baby daughter, she couldn't help smiling. 'The little house is absolutely lovely, Mum' she said. 'So much character.'

Throughout the afternoon grey lines of rain smashed against the window-pane and by five o'clock dusk had fallen. 'What do you expect in November?' said Richard when he arrived back from work. The musty smell of their soggy coats inside the car reminded Nicky of primary school cloakrooms on a wet morning. *But they were going back to Croit Chatreeney.*

Finding the property in the rain and the dark was well-nigh impossible. They drove past the row of brick-built terraced houses several times, until he spotted the hollyhocks, now broken-stemmed and blackened by frost. Nicky's foot squelched on the sodden grass verge as she stepped outside, and the fierce wind flung icy droplets of rain into her face. *Quite exposed,* she thought.

Josh had already opened the front door and once again they were standing in the hallway of *Croit Chatreeney.* Nicky feasted her eyes on every half-remembered detail. Of course, the hallway wasn't the best bit, quite poky actually. Hungry to see the real thing, she opened every door in turn. The living room, with its big bay window, ceramic fireplace and inglenooks either side, was exquisite, although smaller than Nicky remembered, but she'd forgotten about the pea-green melamine units in the kitchen. *Could they paint them, or replace the cupboard doors?* With growing impatience, she flitted from room to room, anticipating the magic of two years ago.

'Thank you,' said Nicky to Josh as their heavy winter shoes clattered down the rustic wooden stairs. 'Sorry to drag you out on a night like this.'

'No problem.' He forced a smile. 'What did you think?'

Richard raised his eyebrows at Nicky.

She took several paces towards the front door, opened it, and set one foot on the doormat outside, before pausing to turn and take one final look. 'Thank you,' she said again, before heading back down the path. The lavender had gone and she couldn't hear the click of the catch above the roaring wind. She shivered as they climbed back into the car. 'Come on. Let's get home.'

'Well?'

'No.'

'What?'

'No.' She fastened her seat belt with a clunk.

'Are you sure?'

'Yes.' She'd lost something that evening, a golden memory broken apart in the November wind.

'I'm so glad,' he said, smiling his square smile. 'It was nice, very nice, and… Okay, if you'd insisted, I would've gone along with it, but the thing is, Nicky, *Croit Chatreeney* is Kate's Cottage. Someone else's house.'

She nodded slowly.

'What I'd like is somewhere that needs doing up, which we can make our own. Nicky and Richard's cottage.'

'You mean... Our house?'

'That's exactly what I mean.'

Life Without Robert

I didn't hear what John said because the soup I was making for our lunch was whirring around in my new food processor. But I could guess.

'Where's Robert?' he said again when I switched it off. He grabbed the packing case my new toy had arrived in, turned it upside down and shook it. A lump of white polystyrene packaging fell to the floor. 'I can't find him. Anywhere.'

'He won't be in there, dear.'

'I want to listen to *The News*.' He was picking things up and putting them down: the toaster, the bread bin, the kettle. 'He was here.'

'You can watch it on the television.'

'I suppose I'll have to, even though I don't like that woman who reads the weather. Horrible voice.' He picked up two dirty coffee mugs, put them into the bowl and turned on the tap, tutting when the almost empty container of detergent spat green splodges on to the side of the sink. In John's opinion the dishwasher didn't do things properly. 'I prefer *Radio Four*.'

'I'm amazed you don't still call it the *Home Service*,' I said to myself as he stomped off.

'Dad's so old-fashioned!' our daughter, Lucy, used to say as a teenager.

And I always said, 'Dad's Dad. We're not going to change him.'

John returned half an hour later, in a grump because the forecast was for 'cold spells with showers'; it would have been different on the radio, obviously. I wished he wouldn't call his ancient Roberts radio 'Robert'. It sounded silly. Childish and silly. Grrr. I shouldn't get irritated with him. We'd been married for over forty years.

'The new food processor's good, isn't it?' I stood up and started clearing away our soup dishes.

'The old one lasted fifteen years. What have you done with it?'

I knew which way this one was going, so I changed the subject. 'We need to go shopping this afternoon.'

'When I've found Robert.' He pulled open the kitchen cupboards one by one, bent down and looked inside.

'He won't be amongst the baked beans. Or the cereal packets.' *I myself should get out of the habit of calling the Roberts radio 'he'.*

He took off his glasses, rubbed them with the tea towel and raised his eyebrows. 'Have you been tidying up and putting things away again?'

'No, dear. As you know, I like the kitchen to be as dirty as possible – like Robert.' I handed him a piece of kitchen paper for more efficient spectacle-cleaning. 'You must admit he's rather scruffy, with tomato ketchup, egg and gravy stains going back several decades.'

'Robert's been with us for a very long time.' He peered behind the microwave. 'I can't believe he would just disappear.'

'He'll turn up.' I shut all the cupboard doors after him, clacketty-clack, like someone stacking deckchairs on the beach. 'While we're in the supermarket, we could look at those digital radios in the electrical section. Sue over the road's got one. She says the signal's much clearer and she can get lots more stations.'

'I only listen to *Radio Four*.' He watched over my shoulder as I opened the fridge: did he suppose Robert might have hidden in the salad boxes? 'Anyway I must write a letter to the Council before we go out.'

'Another one?'

'I want to register my protest.'

'About the Council Tax going up again? They won't take any notice, you know.' I added cucumber and yoghurt to my list.

'But now they're saying I can no longer pay it by cheque.'

'I see. Shall I hand you a quill pen? Or would you prefer a tablet of stone?

'Don't be silly, dear.'

Some minutes later I found him staring at a blank computer in the living room, not typing his letter, but on the internet; I knew which site he would be on without even looking. He gulped down the tea I brought him, his mug clinking against the saucer as he put it down next to the keyboard. 'How can I be secretary of the *Roberts Radio User Group* when I don't even have one?'

'You do have one.'

'Well, where is Robert then?'

'Have you looked in the shed?'

'Yes.'

'The garage?'

'Yes.'

Something caught his attention on screen, a new post on the forum. I imagined the *Roberts Radio User Group* members commiserating with him online. Mumsnet for techies.

He heaved a fierce sigh. 'You've hidden him, haven't you?'

'No, I have not.'

'I know you don't like him.' He spoke without looking at me, his eyes fixed on the screen. 'You say he's dirty.'

'I am not in the habit of throwing your things away, John.'

'What you want is to get rid of Robert, so you can get one of those digital things. Isn't it?

'No, John. It is not.' Seizing my mug, I marched out of the living room and back into the kitchen. The sound it made as I banged it on to the worktop expressed my feelings well. The urge to pick up the telephone hanging on the wall and ring my daughter was almost overwhelming.

114

'Dad's getting so unreasonable,' I could hear myself saying. 'Accusing me of losing things. This isn't the first time.'

'Dad isn't getting any younger, Mum.'

'Don't say that, Lucy. It can't be that. Can it? Not Dad.'

My anger drained from me like poison oozing from a wound. In its place appeared a cloud of fear, little droplets insignificant in themselves but, altogether, capable of suffocating me. I picked up my mug again and examined it: had I cracked it or chipped it? I wished I could retreat into a world where I had no weightier concerns than crockery.

I became aware of John standing in the doorway, his long body casting a shadow in the kitchen. 'I'm sorry,' he said.

I shrugged. 'It's all right.'

'I sometimes get things out of…' He clicked his fingers, once, twice, three times. This gesture and the accompanying snapping sound were confirming my dread. 'I can't think of the word.'

'Proportion.' I got it out as fast as I could. I glimpsed him, as others saw him: a senior citizen, with a stoop, and white hair, although in my mind's eye it was still nut brown and his lined face creased with smiles and laughter. 'Come on. Sit down.'

He slumped on to the wooden kitchen chair, winding his fingers around the wooden ladder-back. 'I need old things, like Robert. I'm no good with new pieces of equipment nowadays. I can cope if everything's familiar. I think.' He lifted his brown eyes to me, as if he had the evening he proposed, a shy man daring himself to look me straight in the eye. 'I need to keep a grip. It's so difficult sometimes.'

I laid my hand on his dry knuckles. 'Let's go and find Robert.'

My Friend Simon

I think this is going to be one of the better places. I have viewed so many.

As I trudge upstairs, the landlord, Miguel, rattles on about rent, and not allowing loud music or pets. He pauses to show me the communal bathroom, muttering something about a plumber coming tomorrow. I don't notice what needs fixing, only that the sink and shower look relatively clean. A yellowing copy of Ernesto Guevara's *Motorcycle Diaries* lies on the lavatory cistern. I wonder how long that's been there.

Miguel stops in front of the room that could be mine. If he'll let me take it. Already, before I've seen inside, I want it. He pushes open the door and I observe that it's bigger than average, with a view from the window which rolls over DF – Distrito Federal – as I've learned to call Mexico City, and beyond to the white peak of Popocatepetl.

'You like?' Miguel fires off the question like a gun.

'Si.'

He takes his mobile from his pocket and reads a text. I shuffle my weight from one foot to the other, fearing that this is another prospective tenant, getting their offer in before mine? Then he asks the usual question. 'Senorita has guarantor? Property-owner here in DF?'

When I shake my head, he shakes his. I should be used to it by now, yet every time searing disappointment washes over me like a wave. I force a smile. 'Thank you for showing me the room.'

As I turn to go, my eyes rest upon the dog-eared, red and black *'No Pasaran'* poster clinging to the door of the neighbouring room, dried-up Blu-tack protruding from under its corners like pale blue boils. Beside it, the father of the Mexican Revolution, Emiliano Zapata, stares down

116

the stairwell from a grainy black and white handbill. The person who put up these posters would have a guarantor in DF.

'Simon's posters,' says Miguel, nodding at them. 'Simon good tenant. *Inglese*.'

A straw of hope, I cling to it. 'Me, English also.' I point to my chest, struggling for words. I used to consider myself fluent in Spanish before I arrived here. 'Language student, at British university. I study in DF. For one year.'

'Simon pay. Every month.' He takes his keys from his pocket to re-lock 'my' room.

'I have money in the bank,' I say. '4,300 pesos. That's the rent, yes? I give you two months, 8,600 pesos. Today.' I long to lie in the cool white bed, sit on the dark wood chair and watch the city through the big window. 'I also good tenant. Me English. Simon English.' I want to add, 'Please, please, let me take that room. I'm so tired and my hotel is so expensive.'

'Go on, Miguel. Let her have it,' calls a male voice from below.

I start. I glance at Miguel. I peer down the stairwell, but see no one.

'She'll be okay. The middle-classes are tediously reliable about such things.'

I wait for the speaker to come clambering up the stairs. I look again at Xavier but he's watching me. Had the voice in my head been wishful thinking? I've been alone for too long, speaking to no one except hotel staff, shopkeepers, bus drivers and potential landlords, sharing no confidences and receiving none, eating every meal alone and feeling no human touch.

'Always. Every month.' This is Miguel speaking; I see his lips move.

'Yes. Yes, I will. Please. Trust me.' I dare to touch the door to the room. I trace the keyhole with my little finger.

He punches his clenched fist into his palm. '8,600 pesos. Today.'

Relief zaps through my body, its tremors juddering down my spine, through the bones in my legs down to my aching feet. 'Si.'

Miguel introduces me to my flatmates when I move in later that day, two men and two women, all Mexican. Talking loud and fast, Fernanda offers me a cigarette and Ana invites me to join them at the bar across the road when I've finished unpacking.

'Yes. That'd be great.' I try to keep the weariness from my voice. 'Where's English Simon?'

'In the south, in Oaxaca,' Miguel says. 'Back soon. Rent day. Next week.'

I stretch out on the white bed, feeling the smooth cotton of the cover against my skin as I watch the Mexican dusk falling like a curtain over my window. I get up and sit on the dark hardwood chair, just for the pleasure of hearing it creak under my weight, but I'm restless, and hungry. I make my way to the shared kitchen, which is not too bad by London student standards. Shoving the unwashed dishes to the back of the worktop, I chop vegetables for my first home-cooked meal in a month. I'm about to toss the onions into the pan when I realise I haven't purchased any cooking oil. I cry out to the stained kitchen wall tiles. 'Stupid woman! *Mujer stupida*.' It sounds better in Spanish.

'You can use mine,' says someone behind me, in English.

Wearing jeans and T-shirt, he's sitting at the kitchen table. I didn't hear him come in.

'On the shelf, right above your head.' The voice is familiar.

'Hey, you're…' I turn around to face him. 'Thanks so much for putting a word in for me earlier.'

He shrugs.

'You must be Simon. I'm Isabel.'

'I know.' He points to the shelf again. 'Help yourself to herbs and spices. I don't need them anymore.'

'I'm so grateful to you. I didn't know what I was going to do. I will keep up to date with the rent, you know.'

He holds up his hand. 'Can we talk about something else now?'

I expect him to pose the normal questions travellers put to each other. What I am doing in DF? Where do I live in England? When he doesn't ask, I tell him anyway. 'We had to fight for our Mexico placement, you know. The university authorities, they wanted to pack all the students on our course off to Madrid and bung us in a hall of residence. Together. Cassie and I, we wanted to go somewhere we could integrate with local people.'

'Where's Cassie now?'

'She flew back home after three days. She couldn't cope with it.'

He nodded, his body rocking with the motion of his head. 'So you're here on your own.'

'I can manage. I am managing, aren't I? What do you do?'

'I've been in DF for five years.'

'What do you do?'

'Do?' he repeats after me.

'Yes.'

'I've been in Oaxaca, supporting the striking teachers.'

'Yes, but what do you do for a living?'

He raises his eyebrows until they merge into his shaggy bleached fringe. 'I used to be a student like you. Once. At Oxford. Not that I learned anything of value there. The university of life, Isabel, that's the greatest educator.' His smile creases the freckles on his tanned face. 'But, as you seem very keen to pigeon-hole me economically, I used to give English lessons.'

'I see.'

'I'm an Anarchist, Isabel. Everyone brings to the table what they can.' He stands up. 'I'd better go.'

'Will you be at the bar with the others? I want to buy you a drink.'

'Thanks, but I'm meeting my friend, Ernesto. I need to get his book from the bathroom.'

'Okay. Bye then. It was nice to talk in English.'

'I thought you wanted to integrate with the locals.'

'Yes, but...'

He rolls his eyes and grins. He hovers, wrapping his hands around the lintel. 'Was it cold in England?'

'No-o. It was July when I left.'

He pulls himself up on the doorframe, lifting his feet from the floor. 'I've forgotten what being cold is like.'

I eat my meal, the sounds of my spoon against my bowl rattling through the empty house. I listen out for footsteps, a door being opened and closed, a toilet being flushed perhaps, but I hear nothing. Later I join my new flatmates at the bar; Ana and Fernanda pull another chair up to their table and order me horchata. They're friendly but I struggle to follow their Latino Spanish. I keep hoping that Simon, who I spot drinking at a bar across the road, will join us, but he's engrossed in conversation with a bloke wearing a beret. He doesn't return to our place to sleep.

'Miguel, Miguel. What are you doing? I've just arrived back from the university at lunchtime and he is tearing down Simon's posters, shreds of red and black dropping upon the stone floor.

He doesn't reply.

'Miguel. No. These are Simon's posters.' I peer down the

corridor, hoping one of my roommates will burst from his or her door, but, in the late afternoon, when the rain falls, they are out at work. 'Simon's a good tenant. Simon always pays rent.'

'Simon never pay rent again.'

'Yes, he will.'

'No, Isabel, never.' Miguel takes out another cigarette and lights it. 'Shot by police, in Oaxaca. Last Thursday. His father in England, he telephone me. They come, his parents. To DF. Next Monday.'

I gulp. Young people don't die, do they?

He rips down Emilio Zapata, the sound of tearing paper ricocheting down the corridor and back.

'Don't, Miguel. Please.'

'It's all right, Isabel,' says a voice behind me. 'He needs to re-let the room.'

'Simon.' I reach out to grab him, but my hand goes through nothingness, hitting the wall with a painful thud.

Then he's gone.

Back in my own room, I stand stiff and motionless in the middle of the floor, my hands pressed against my ears in a vain attempt to blot out the noise in the corridor, but it throbs through the white bruise forming upon my knuckle.

'Sorry I upset you.'

I spin around. 'You?'

Simon, he's here, cross-legged on my rug, bronzed hairy legs folded over one another, knobbly toes showing through flip-flops.

'How did you get in?' I'm sure I closed the bedroom door behind me. I must be imagining things. Too much stress over the last few weeks. 'Are you... Are you real?'

'What's real? I left that sort of question behind me at Oxford.'

'You know what I mean. You'd better tell Miguel. He thinks you're dead.'

121

'I am dead.'

'But you look real.'

'That word again.'

Again I stretch out my hand to touch him but he shakes his head slowly. I withdraw it.

'Do you mind me being here? I couldn't bear it in Oaxaca any longer. They were putting flowers in the road where it happened.'

'But you know the others – Fernanda and Ana – better. And what about your friend, Ernesto.'

'I see Ernesto all the time. Trouble is, Isabel, I'm homesick.'

'You?'

'For the last few months, I've been dreaming about thatched cottages, warm beer, and cream teas. I was saving up for the plane fare home, but I didn't make much money giving English lessons.'

'Your parents, when they come, they'll take you back to the UK?'

'No.'

'Really?'

'Too expensive and too many regulations. They're organising a funeral in the Anglican cathedral here in DF, to reunite me with the God I've neglected all my life, then burying me in the cathedral graveyard.'

'Oh Simon. What are you going to do?'

'Do? I can't do anything. But, please Isabel, talk to me about England. In English. For the little time I have left.'

Provided I steer him off politics, he's great company.

Simon's father is in the lobby, speaking broken Spanish to Miguel. His mother hovers outside Simon's empty room, her face pale and pinched, with red chafing around her eyes. I make her a cup of tea. She tells me about Simon as a little boy and a teenager, how he picked up some 'funny ideas' at Oxford. 'We had some arguments, but none of that matters anymore. He loved Mexico, you know, never wanted to go back to England.'

When I return to my room, he's sprawled over the floor as usual. 'Simon, your mother and father are here. Go and talk to them.'

He holds out his hands. 'I can't, Isabel.'

'Appear to them as you do to me.'

'My mother would freak. She's got a heart condition.'

'It's your only chance. Of getting back to England, I mean.'

His bleached shaggy hair swings around his face as he shakes his head again. 'My parents, they're not easy to talk to.'

'Come on.' I open the door, pushing it against its hinges, as if to usher him out, but his silhouette merges into the white-washed wall. 'Simon!' I throw myself on to my bed, crying out in frustration.

I know he'll be back.

'But you can go anywhere you like,' I say when he reappears just minutes later. 'Can't you? You got yourself from Oaxaca to DF?'

He doesn't answer.

'Your body will stay in the grave in DF, but you – the real you, the bit of you I'm seeing now – can go home to England.' My words tumble over each other, melting into the thin DF air.

His leg makes no sound as he stretches it across the rush matting on my floor. All his movements are silent.

'Can't it? I mean, can't you?' I wait, without breathing, listening for the intake of breath which begins all human speech.

But obviously there's no breath. His words themselves

break the silence. 'I travelled from Oaxaca by bus. The driver was one of the comrades.' His forehead creases into two ridged arches. 'Not sure I could do all the way across the Atlantic, though. I think I have to have someone I know with me.'

'Your mum and dad.'

'I suppose.'

'Try it, Simon. Try it.'

'Okay. Okay. I'll try.' The frown on his brow tightens. 'Would you be all right? Here in DF by yourself?'

'Yes, of course.'

'Let's be honest. You weren't coping a week or so ago.'

'No, but…' I look around my room, at my phone lying on my bed and my Diesel jeans slung over the chair. 'I'm okay now.'

'Sure?'

'Yes.' Through my open window, I hear the chink-chink of glasses at the bar where later I'm meeting Ana and Fernanda. 'I'll miss you though.'

'I'll miss you too.'

'But we'll see each other in London next summer.' I pause to make my point. 'Won't we?'

He nods.

The Lorry Drivers' Book Club

I don't want to talk about Ellie. Here we are, Jez, Frank and I, sitting around our usual table in Des's Café and I just want to enjoy it. We've finished lunch, Des's chips and cheese, the best on the road, and we're lounging back in our chairs as we drink our tea. We drivers like our bevvies in mugs, piping hot and mahogany brown, and with more sugar lumps than we can count. Chips, the drone of traffic outside and my mates, that's what I need. The last few weeks have been Hell.

But Frank's getting out his copy of *Jane Eyre* and thumping it down on the table, amongst smears of tomato ketchup. 'Book Club.'

'No,' I say. 'No.'

Jez tweaks his lank grey ponytail, as greasy as Des's chips. 'Book Club was Ellie's thing and Ellie's not here.'

Frank used to moan and whinge, saying books were for 'birds'. He'd meet Ellie's eye as he said it, his eyebrows raised as a challenge, after sneaking a glance at the contours of her ample boobs under her overall. Ellie was one of the boys: short brown hair, sturdily built, with bulging biceps. She handled her rig like a man and could turn it around on a postage stamp.

She used to answer with a grin, a 'So what?' and 'What's your problem?' sort of grin. 'More male writers get published than female.' She said this so often that Jez and I would say it for her.

We go back a long way, Jez, Frank and me, messing around at school and leaving with nothing by way of qualifications. Jez and I used to be like Frank about the Book Club, but over the months the reading has grown on us, because Ellie had a way of making it interesting.

But that was then.

125

I slide my plate away from me, knocking Frank's copy of *Jane Eyre* on to the dirty floor, wet from the imprints of drivers' boots since dawn this morning.

'She'd want us to carry on.' Frank uses his sleeve to wipe mud off the cover. He meets my eye. 'What did you do that for, Dave?'

'She would want us to carry on.' Jez pulls his own copy from his pocket.

I lean forward. 'How can either of you say what a girl would want when she's lying in a cold grave?'

'Look…' says Jez. Jez is the gentlest bloke imaginable, a right softie, so what comes next chills me inside. 'No disrespect to Ellie. If I found the bloke who did what he did to her. You see that bridge over there?' Jez nods through the window. Des's Café is at the exit for Witham in Essex and, to access the town, you cross the carriageway over a long concrete bridge. 'I'd take him on there… dangle him over the edge. Make him squirm. Scream. Plead. Then he'd slip through my fingers and… drop.'

I exchange looks with Frank. He shakes his head in tiny movements. The men from the next table stop talking and raise their heads. One of them swivels around to face us. 'The police are saying she probably knew her attacker.'

'They always say that,' I say. When no one else speaks, I feel the need to fill the silence. 'She was in that lay-by by herself. Must've been some nutter. She was a few miles from Clacket Lane Services. Don't know why she didn't just stay in the lorry park.' *Shut up, Dave. Shut up.*

Silence again. After a moment, Frank lays his hand on Jez's arm. 'I'd do the same, mate.'

'Yeah.' I'm staring through the window at the bridge, at the cars, lorries and buses pounding underneath it, kicking up sodden muck and spraying it at the once white concrete pillars. I need to change the subject. 'All right then. Book Club. *Jane Eyre.*'

126

'At last.' Frank jabs his copy with his finger. 'That *Mr Rochester* was a right plonker.'

Jez nods. 'It was the mad woman who got to me. Those red eyes. And her prowling around and setting fire to everything. I couldn't stop thinking about her all the way up the A1.'

'Horror film stuff,' says Frank.

Despite everything I want to join in and I do for a bit, but then they move on to horror films in general, which isn't Book Club at all. 'Ellie would've said something really clever,' says Jez, with a sigh, as I stand up to go.

Three weeks ago, she said it. Ellie had a loud voice, the sort that carried across the lorry parks. I was clambering out my cab at Clacket Lane Service Station in Surrey when I heard her call, 'Dave, me old mate.' We chatted over mugs of builders' tea, chips and jam, she not being the sort to worry about weight. She was different without Jez and Frank being around: softer, gentler. She said she hadn't managed to visit her hairdresser recently, so her gingery brown hair was growing in loose curls from her mannish crop, and I noticed light freckles showing through her pale delicate skin. '*Jane Eyre* was my favourite book as a kid,' she said, 'but I didn't understand it until I re-read it last year.' She talked for half an hour, explaining things about characters and events which I'd never noticed.

'Ellie, you're really clever. You could be a teacher or something.'

She laughed. 'Done that. Too much marking, too much Ofsted. Driving's not bad money. And it gives me headspace.'

'Uh?'

'I like to think.'

'Uh?'

'I'm a writer, Dave.' She lowered her voice and cast her eyes around the cafe, as if checking that the other trucker heads were sufficiently deep in their ketchup troughs. 'I've had short stories published. And I'm writing a novel. I think while I'm driving and write when I lay off for the night.' She blushed as she met my eyes. 'Not all writers are rich. I need my day job. I'm on my own. Single. Like *Jane Eyre*.'

According to Charlotte Bronte, *Jane Eyre* was plain. Ellie was not.

'I'm too tired to write tonight. I'm going to watch a DVD in my cab. Like to join me? There's a lay-by a few miles from here. I don't want to pay overnight parking charges at Clacket Lane and I'm sure you don't.'

This is where I got everything wrong.

Jez and Frank are getting up from the table now. Jez asks where I'm heading, but I don't answer. I'm going to save him some trouble.

I take the Witham exit and stop on the bridge. I lean over the balustrade, watching the traffic. I do try. I imagine how it'd be, landing on the roof of a truck, being shaken off into the oncoming traffic, cars swerving, brakes screeching.

I can't do it.

About the Author

Rosemary Johnson has had short stories and flash fiction published in *CaféLit*, *Fiction on the Web*, *Friday Flash Fiction*, *Paragraph Planet*, *The Copperfield Review*, *Scribble* and *Radgepacket*, and broadcast on *Hannah's Bookshelf* (North Manchester FM). She is a member of the Association of Christian Writers (until recently responsible for the ACW website) and she reviews books for *Together* (trade magazine for the Christian publishing industry).

Rosemary loves reading and started writing at a very young age because her favourite authors hadn't written enough books to keep her occupied. A history graduate, she particularly enjoys writing historical fiction and her novel, *Wodka, Or Tea With Milk*, set during the Solidarity period in Poland in the 1980s, is published by The Conrad Press. Rosemary blogs at
https://rosemaryreaderandwriter.wordpress.com/

Provenance of the Stories

Rosemary Johnson's stories have appeared in *CaféLit* over a number of years:

An Important Call	January 2020
Eight O'Clock (as Half Past Eight)	May 2019
The Witch	September 2020
Looking for Our House	Oct 2019
Ella's Holiday (also in Best of CaféLit 4)	March 2014
Running Away	January 2019
Penny Carter is Unwell	April 2011
Not Working (also in Best of CafeLit12)	June 2022
Puss in Boots	December 2022
What's in a Name	March 2022
The Black Sheep's Haunts	December 2021
Pavlova	September 2022
My Pizza	December 2020

Not all these stories appear in this short story collection. Maybe in the next?

The following stories were first published as follows:

Bachelor Boy *A Long Short Story* (ezine, no longer online) – 2015

Unaccustomed as I Am *A Word in Your Ear* (http://www.awordinyourear.org.uk/) – 2020

Daniel and the Pussycats *The Copperfield Review* (*The Copperfield Review* historical fiction magazine is no longer online) – 2013

Kitty's Infernal Machine *Stories in the Ether* (Steampunk ezine, no longer online) – 2011

Not a Proper Evacuee *The Copperfield Review* – 2019

Anna the Dissident *Circa* (historical fiction ezine, no longer online) – 2013

Tomatoes and Their Part in Brexit *Alfie Dog Fiction* (https://alfiedog.com) – 2017

Never Too Old, Never Too Young *Scribble* (print magazine, published by Park Publications) – 2020

Last Hot Chocolate in Mostar *Youth Imagination* (ezine, no longer online) – _2015

The Lorry Drivers Book Club Published by *Fiction Junkies* (https://www.fictionjunkies.com/) – 2021

My Blue Period Published by *Fiction Junkies* (https://www.fictionjunkies.com/) – 2021

Burnt Down *Alfie Dog Fiction* (https://alfiedog.com) – 2016

My Friend Simon *An Earthless Melting Pot* (print magazine, ISBN 9781514171196) – 2015

Life Without Robert *Words* (print magazine, ISSN 0961-6985) – 2012

Like to Read More Work Like This?

Then sign up to our mailing list and download our free collection of short stories, *Magnetism*. Sign up now to receive this free e-book and also to find out about all of our new publications and offers.

Sign up here:
http://eepurl.com/gbpdVz

Please Leave a Review

Reviews are so important to writers. Please take the time to review this book. A couple of lines is fine.

Reviews help the book to become more visible to buyers. Retailers will promote books with multiple reviews.

This in turn helps us to sell more books... And then we can afford to publish more books like this one.

Leaving a review is very easy.

Go to https://amzn.to/4mnz7o3, scroll down the left-hand side of the Amazon page and click on the 'Write a customer review' button.

Other Writing by Rosemary Johnson

Wodka, or Tea with Milk
Published by The Conrad Press

Wodka, or Tea with Milk takes the reader on an immersive, rollercoaster ride into the Solidarnosc years in 1980s Poland. Marya Weiclawski is second-generation British, the daughter of Polish refugees who fled during World War Two. When her Cambridge University interview goes wrong – her fault actually – she resolves to seek out her Polish family whom no one speaks of, and her father's RAF comrade, Pyotr Murkowski, whom her beloved dad, Jerzy, has suddenly stopped talking about. Marya becomes involved in the shipyard strikes in Gdansk in 1980 and falls in love with Jan, a shipyard worker. Jan is well liked by colleagues, unflappable and down-to-earth - a bit too much so for volatile Marya – but he appears to have no family and in Poland family is everything.

'Loved reading this book, so interesting the way the true history weaves through the story line. I learnt about Polish history as well enjoying a good story.' (*Amazon*)

Order from Amazon:

Paperback: ISBN 978-1-915494-67-2
eBook: ASIN B0CH7BZYTD

Other Publications by Bridge House

Once We Were Heroes
by Henry Lewi

Where do the gods of Olympus do their shopping?

Do the Old Gods live amongst us, and if so where? And which jobs do they do? Where do the Old Gods shop, or do they do it online? Which football clubs do they support? When Angels are sent down to Earth, how do they get home? How did Vampires cope with Lockdown during the pandemic? And finally, are Extra-Terrestrials dangerous, or do they just want to speak to us?

'Henry Lewi writes with confidence and with imagination. The story about the gods moving to North London provided an interesting opportunity to comment on modern times. The Pandemic features in many of the items in the collection.'
(Amazon)

Order from Amazon:

Paperback: ISBN 978-1-914199-82-0
eBook: ISBN 978-1-914199-83-7

Blood and Electricity
by Steven John

'*We took an excursion around the sun again this year, five hundred million miles back to where we started.*' From *A Brief History of Time in Our House*, a story in this collection.

There are no UFOs or extra-terrestrials in this first collection of short stories and flash fiction by Steven John. *Blood and Electricity* is about the vital currents that flow through and around us, powering our lonely orbits of life. We are all bright stars that appear close to one another when viewed with the naked eye, but the truth is, we're separated by incomprehensible distances.

'This is a tremendous collection of flash fiction. Steven John is a master of words, but also so able to write situations and characters with which we immediately identify.' *(Amazon)*

Order from Amazon:

Paperback: ISBN 978-1-914199-80-6
eBook: ISBN 978-1-914199-81-3

Something Very Human
by Hannah Retallick

This collection takes the reader on a journey through life, from the innocence of young voices to the reflections of those seeking meaning as they look back at the paths they've taken.

Each story captures the very essence of being human. The characters tackle everyday challenges, face inner struggles, navigate familial relationships and friendships, fall in love and out of love, process grief, and reflect on the beautiful fragility of it all.

Something Very Human is the debut short story collection from award-winning writer, Hannah Retallick.

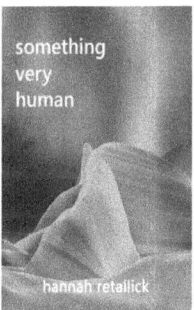

'This was quite a collection of unputdownable short stories. Except I needed to take a break after each one to savour the impact and not move on too quickly!' *(Amazon)*

Order from Amazon:

Paperback: ISBN 978-1-914199-76-9
eBook: ISBN 978-1-914199-77-6